Praise for the *Cooked to Death* Series

"An eclectic smorgasbord of storytelling talent."
—Laurie Hertzel, *Star Tribune*

"*Cooked to Death* is a tasty companion whether you're traveling by plane with hours in the air or waiting on the ground. Or you could read it in one sitting while eating your favorite food. (Make sure you check for poison first, just to be sure . . .)"
—Mary Ann Grossmann, *Pioneer Press*

"There's everything from flat-out humor to the downright malevolent, and free-ranging foul play in between."
—Ethan Boatner, *Lavender Magazine*

"An entertaining ride for all the senses—including taste! The corresponding recipes provided after each thriller offered continued satisfaction."
—Kara Doucette, *Yelp Twin Cities* senior community manager and marketing director

"*Cooked to Death Volume 2* is a fun, surprising book that serves up a heaping helping of mystery and detail. Each author has a unique writing style that keeps the reader guessing. What really makes this book a fun experience is the tasty recipes that are included inside. Not only are the recipes delicious, but the stories are intriguing and will keep you on your toes."
—Erin Campbell,
Food Network Holiday Baking Champion
and *Food Network Star* finalist

"This second culinary collection offers a tantalizing smorgasbord of terrific stories with great recipes on the side. From the deliciously dark to the fluffy and funny, there's something here that will satisfy the literary appetite of every reader. Buy it now and indulge yourself tonight."
—William Kent Krueger

D1368394

VOLUME II

COOKed TO DeatH:

Edited by RHONDA GILLILAND

LYiNg ON a PlatE

WISE *Ink*
CREATIVE ★ PUBLISHING

ISBN: 978-1-63489-082-3
eISBN: 978-1-63489-083-0

Library of Congress Catalog Number 2017947404

Printed in the United States of America
First Printing: 2017

21   20   19   18   17   5   4   3   2   1

Cover design by Jessie Sayward Bright
Illustrations by Bonnie Planque

Wise Ink Creative Publishing
837 Glenwood Ave.
Minneapolis, MN 55405
www.wiseinkpub.com

Menu

PREFACE

Rhonda Gilliland   1

APPETIZERS

The Overlook - Tom Combs   4

Cracked - Michelle Kubitz   9

Kitchen Matters - Lori L. Lake   21

SALAD

Sweet Justice - Brian Lutterman   42

Cupcake Battle Royale - Brian Landon   52

Blueberry Bliss - Cathlene Buchholz   65

SOUP

Serving Up a Surprise - Marlene Chabot   82

The Way to a Man's Heart - Wendy Webb   94

The Debut of Reggie Smalls - Michael Sears   107

ENTREES

Circle of Life - Kristi Belcamino   122

Wolfie - Christine Husom   131

Love, Lobster, and Lies - Nancy Tesler   142

DESSERTS

Death at Pinewood Manor - Marilyn Rausch   160

Eat, Pray, and Maybe Die - Colin Nelson   169

Whole Lotta Bull - Susan Koefod   180

ABOUT THE AUTHORS   197

Recipes

Deviled Eggs   8

Scrambled Eggs   19

Gloria's Oven Omelet   20

Lori's Criminally Tasty Frittata Recipe   39

Mounds Bars   51

Raspberry Arsenic Swirl Cupcakes   63

Blueberry Bliss Pie   78

Chicken Wild Rice Soup   93

Elizabeth's Harvest Stew   105

Lobster Macaroni Salad   120

Kyatchi's Hot Dogs   130

Shrimp and Artichokes in Wine   141

Lobster Flambé in Whiskey   157

Mrs. Potter's Flourless Chocolate Torte   168

Banana Chocolate Curry Pecan Bread   179

Crossroads Delicatessen Peanut Logs   196

 # *Preface*

BY RHONDA GILLILAND

WHO KNEW how this foodie anthology would catch on fire? The original open submission was a chance for never-before-published and seasoned authors to share their passion for crime and cooking. We invited the best mystery writers the Twin Cities had to offer, and three from out of state. *Cooked to Death Volume II* has the same formula with all-new authors and recipes. It was a way to show off their family recipes and introduce readers to fabulous local chefs and restaurants.

In *Volume II* each section has a small, medium, and large story. Some are using a familiar protagonist from their own series—you may recognize Brian Lutterman's Pen Wilkenson, Susan Koefod's Arvo Thorson, or Nancy Tesler's Carrie Carlin. Others, such as Wendy Webb and Lori L. Lake, are using this to showcase new characters. The rest are stand-alones.

The recipes are entertaining as well. For example, Keys Cafe doesn't use measurements. Twin Cities local celebrity baker and writer, Danny Klecko, gives us another unique baked good. While I didn't submit a story, I featured my famous deviled eggs and my Grandmother's lobster macaroni salad. Many of the authors were just as excited to share a recipe as well as another thrilling mystery. It turns out that food and crime do mix. I want to thank Michael Allan Mallory for giving me the key to solo edit the second in the series. Eat up.

—Rhonda Gilliland, Editor

Appetizers

The Overlook

BY TOM COMBS

EVERYTHING SHE DID bothered him.

When she ate, she made smacking sounds and tiny whistling noises as her lips flared for each new bite. She could eat a grape and make it sound like a hyena gutting a zebra.

He'd considered that she did it to annoy him, but that would be giving her too much credit. She was unaware of anything beyond herself. Self-absorption was more than an unfortunate part of her personality—it was her world.

His feelings were like the molten, spitting magma hidden deep beneath the earth's surface. No one knew.

"Geez, you look good this morning, babe. Are you up for a hike?"

"Sounds boring." She delivered her dismissive utterance without interrupting her focus on the first of her multiple daily flossing rituals. Her face was contorted and her upper teeth exposed. *Plink! Plink!* The floss twanged off each successive tooth like someone plucking the world's most obnoxious banjo.

"Autumn on the North Shore of Lake Superior—it's a beautiful day. I know a special place."

"Bright sun today—you know about UV rays and my skin." She paused her dental manipulations and put a hand to her cheek, leaning close to the mirror.

"Don't you have some of that four-hundred-dollars-an-ounce cocoa-butter-sheep-placenta-aloe sunblock you bought? Besides, if you don't get exercise, your glutes might lose tone. "

She turned and checked her Givenchy-shorts-covered ass in the full-length mirror of their luxury suite. "Well, maybe—"

"That's my beauty. Slap on some sunscreen and we'll take the Jaguar up to Split Rock Lighthouse."

The top-of-the-line Jaguar she just had to have. Never a moment's thought about how much insurance he'd had to shill to pay for it.

Selling insurance. He sighed. The money was great, but the job required him to kiss so much ass he needed diaper cream for lip balm.

But it did establish my belief in big policies.

"I know of an incredible trail, and the exercise will more than match one of your spin classes with Bradford or your circuit training with Marquis." *Actually, it might not equal the "full" workout, bitch.*

She turned from the mirror, her freshly tweezed eyebrows raised. "I didn't know you knew my trainers' names." She did not meet his eyes.

"Oh, heck yeah, great guys. Just saw them the other day." He'd seen and heard them on the high resolution digital recording the private investigator captured. The field of view had included all three of them at the motel. He'd nearly vomited.

"Toss your things together. I'll pick you up at the lodge's entry. I had the chef pack a basket of gourmet treats for us." *Ah, the loving husband doting on his beautiful wife.* He'd also made dinner reservations and ordered a magnum of champagne for their room tonight. Clear evidence of a thoughtful and loving husband planning special time with his wife.

The three-mile-long trail started alongside the great lake and ascended a series of switchbacks toward the overlook high above. The North Shore's fall leaves shimmered, a tapestry of pigments unlike any other. The climb involved some serious work and the route was little traveled because of the difficulty.

Today he felt so jazzed he floated up the switchbacks. He could've put her unfaithful, narcissistic self on his back with the chef's pack of picnic goodies and double-timed it.

Every step brought them closer to his spot. The special place at the cliff's edge where the land ended and one could stand with gulls circling beneath while Lake Superior's waves smashed against the rocks more than two hundred feet below.

He'd visited the site years earlier and the combination of majesty, danger, and solitude had stuck in his mind.

As he advanced toward the pinnacle, his course now led over bare granite with no traces of trail or plant life remaining. He reached the edge and peered over the sheer drop. His chest tightened. The sight and sound of the violent collision of water on rocks far below inspired awe.

Separated from the cliff face by a two-foot span stood the broad top of a freestanding chimney of rock—solid and separate. The magnificent perch was an adventurer's dream for a dramatic photo. This was the place. He stood and positioned himself, his breath coming fast.

She loved to be photographed, had no fear of heights, and was sure-footed. A natural athlete with a magic body—beautiful on the outside. *Such a waste.*

"Look, honey. Isn't it spectacular?" The gulls wheeled below, their calls reminding him of her cries on the private investigator's recording. The sun shone golden, the air was crisp, and the fall colors were vibrant. *. . . God, she truly is gorgeous.*

He held up his camera-phone.

"If you step across and stand there I can get an amazing shot. Be careful." She moved alongside him; he smelled Chanel and cocoa butter. He readied himself, his heart hammering. It needed to be done.

· · · · ·

The body launched out and away, arms wind-milling, trying to reclaim equilibrium that no longer mattered. Their eyes linked for a frozen instant.

The cries of the gulls ceased as the mass hurtled past. The abrupt, meaty sound of the impact penetrated the distance and the rumble of crashing waves.

Pitiless eyes peered over the edge at the destruction that had resulted from the explosive collision of flesh and rock.

She backed away from the cliff's edge.

She took out her cell phone, then dialed 911.

"Oh, my God!" She paused, knowing she'd nailed the hysterical note dead on. "My husband! Oh, my God. He's fallen . . . " She disconnected. The GPS link would bring the rescue personnel to her.

It would take time for them to arrive. Taking out her sunscreen, she applied a bit more, taking care to get the area around her eyes. That was the zone her dermatologist said was particularly prone to damage.

She retrieved the pack, then peered into the basket within.

Hmmm, looks tasty.

DEVILED EGGS

Courtesy of Rhonda Gilliland

INGREDIENTS

- 12 hard-cooked eggs
- 4 tbsp. mayo
- 1 tsp. yellow mustard
- 1 tbsp. sweet relish
- 1 tsp. horseradish or horseradish sauce

DIRECTIONS

Split eggs in half lengthwise and remove yolks. In a bowl mash yolks very well with a fork or pastry blender. Add the rest. Stir together until smooth. Adjust if needed. Fill whites using a teaspoon. Sprinkle with paprika for looks. Cover with plastic wrap. Serve chilled.

Cracked

BY MICHELLE KUBITZ

JARRET'S FIRST ATTEMPT at making scrambled eggs wasted half a carton and ended a scorched mess in Grandma Janet's best non-stick pan.

That was nearly a year ago, but Jarret could still remember it: the eggs cold from the carton, smooth in his palm. Jarret was missing Mama, thinking about her—the way she'd raise her hand slightly, the soft thwack of eggshell as it struck the edge of the countertop. Mama never made a mess, somehow timing the snick of the shell with a closely followed fluid motion, separating it at the perfect moment.

Jarret had already cracked the initial egg before he remembered that Mama put them into a bowl first. But the gas was already on under Grandma's skillet, so Jarret dumped the first egg and grabbed the second one. That one smooshed, leaving shattered shells and clear yellow goo on the edge of Grandma's painfully neat granite countertops. The clear stuff piddled down the front of the oak cabinets and dribbled onto the spotless white tile below.

"I just scrubbed those cupboards." As if equipped with radar for such disasters, Grandma Janet materialized out of nowhere, surveying the scene of her once spotless culinary kingdom, thin lips white with disapproval.

A year later, Jarret remembered the mad whir of the stove's hood as it tried but failed to keep up with the smell of scorched eggs.

"You sonofabitch," she had grated, giving Jarret the look she reserved for the men in her life and piles of dog crap she found in the front yard. Jarret dropped his gaze—and Grandma's spatula—as her angry Nordic blue eyes blazed over the mess. The next thing he saw was Grandma's lacquered beige talons sinking into both sides of his chin. Mama's eyes could throw sparks when she was mad, but Grandma Janet's were a batch of blue fireworks.

"I hate you." Grandma's voice was a choke and a sob. "You killed my baby!"

Pastor Brad Forland darted a look at Harmon Earling's left hand. The ring finger was shorn clean away, the middle and index fingers gone above the second knuckle. Brad studied the missing fingers and fought an inane urge to ask Harmon how he had lost them.

You're in trouble when the safest conversation starter is about a person's lost fingers.

Brad looked up when Harmon chuckled, his face reddening, utterly busted staring at the older man's hand.

"I was a machinist," the man said dryly, his tone and inflection full of the vowels that identified him as one of the second-generation Norwegian Americans in the town. "Some jerkalot wasn't paying attention and got me while I was setting up his lathe." Harmon flexed the remaining fingers. "Bypassed the automatic shutdown to turn it on and gave me an early retirement." Earling bowed his head, the light from the dining room pendant above catching patches of scalp through the cloudy gray hair kept in a comb over. "He thought I had finished what I was doing."

"That's . . ." Brad let his thought trail off. It didn't matter what he had been taught in seminary about counseling his parishioners; no amount of psychology classes or seminars had prepared him for a family like this. A year before, Brad thought his biggest challenge at Good Shepherd Lutheran Church was a dwindling congregation comprised of blue-hairs and Baby Boomers. Good Shepherd was one of three Lutheran churches located in Hawick, a stagnant town of 4,000 in southwestern Minnesota. God had sent Brad to grow his congregation and give people a reason to come to church again. To amp up attendance beyond the handful of parishioners who faithfully made their way to the pews on Sunday mornings. But nothing had prepared Brad for what he had walked into after his installation at Good Shepherd. The two a.m. phone call that woke him from a dead sleep. He had thought it was some sort of Halloween prank, but it was the county sheriff's department, who needed Brad to come with their deputies to make a death notification to one of his parishioners. And that's how Brad officially met Harmon and Janet Earling.

Between last Halloween and this Indian summer day in late September, Harmon Earling had lost somewhere around 25 pounds that he hadn't needed to lose. It wasn't immediately noticeable unless you took a long look at the man's face and how his skin seemed to puddle wherever gravity pulled it.

Brad cleared his throat, "That's a bad injury." Brad tipped up his coffee cup. He had been sitting in the Earling house for nearly half an hour and had barely touched it, beyond a polite first sip that told of too much water and too few grounds, followed by a couple halfhearted sips to fill awkward silences.

Brad had the cup halfway to his mouth when he heard a clinking in the kitchen—some utensil against a bowl, he guessed. An ordinary enough sound, but Brad suddenly wished that his back wasn't toward the kitchen door. It was Jarret Hartung, the Earlings' grandson. Although Harmon assured Brad that the sixteen-year-old was harmless, Jarret wasn't the gawky teenager that Brad met during his first weeks as Good Shepherd's minister. While Harmon diminished, Jarret seemingly doubled in body mass until he was roughly the size of an NFL linebacker.

Harmon looked across the dining room to the three-season porch where Janet Earling sat on a couch, staring out past their yard at a dying cornfield. "Thank you for coming today," Harmon said. "We can't leave Jarret by himself anymore, he's just . . ."

Brad cleared his throat and pushed the brochure that Harmon handed to him across the table, wondering, not for the first time, why the healthcare industry preferred pastel colors for their marketing materials. Reassuring stock photos of happy-looking people, young and old, dotted the brochure's glossy cover.

Brad hoped he wasn't lying when he said, "This is for the best."

• • • • •

Two eggs. A splash of milk. Jarret grabbed a fork from the dish drainer and whisked until the eggs turned a foamy pale yellow that matched Grandma Janet's kitchen walls. Before she left, Jarret's big sister Mallory tried to teach him what she remembered about Mama's scrambled eggs. Mama didn't want any brown bits on her eggs—every bite had to be an unblemished, fluffy yellow. It took Mallory and Jarret a few tries and about a dozen eggs before they figured out Mama's secret. Constant motion—Mama kept the eggs, spatula, and pan moving as soon as the eggs started to coagulate.

All the eggs needed after that was salt and pepper. Mama kept a small open bowl of kosher salt on the back of the stove and bought tri-color peppercorns to grind fresh. No table salt or glass containers of ageless black pepper would suffice in Mama's kitchen. Depending on what kind of day Dad was having, he'd either tell Mama she should've been on a cooking show or say Mama was being fancy again. The way that Dad said "fancy" was the same way people talked about unexpected car repairs or doctor's visits.

Those kinds of days used to make Jarret's stomach hurt. Those were the days Mallory whispered that they'd be better off if their folks would just get a divorce. But Jarret didn't want that. He didn't want to be like his friend Alex, who had to spend one weekend with his mom and her crappy boyfriend, then the next at his dad's tiny apartment above the town laundromat.

Jarret's hands faltered as he grabbed Mama's old skillet. Mallory was gone. Alex had stopped talking to him shortly after Christmas. And Jarret really didn't like to think about his parents. But sometimes he had to talk about them—to people like Dr. Zachary at his appointments in Castleton, or when Grandpa made him talk to Pastor Brad. He didn't mind talking to Dr. Zachary—her questions made sense. She was trying to help him get over and deal with what had happened over the last year. Pastor Brad should have been cool, he was the youngest pastor in town, but Jarret didn't like the pastor's questions—they made him feel stupid.

Jarret shook his head to clear it and started in on the eggs again, turning the range up on high after he heard the *snick-snick-snick-WHOOSH* of the gas burner. Jarret reached up for the cooking spray, ignoring the t-shaped scar that started under the base of his palm and ended in a hook halfway to his elbow. It looked like a purplish-red crucifix, tender and still healing some six months after he'd carved it there. It didn't even hurt, but it was ugly—the pastor seemed to stare at it every time Jarret sat across from him in the man's office. He didn't like to talk about his scar either.

Jarret gave the eggs a final whisk with the fork and dumped them into the skillet. It only took a few seconds for the underside of the eggs to start cooking. Grabbing Mama's favorite spatula, Jarret grabbed the handle of the frying pan and scraped the cooked eggs off the bottom of the pan, flipping them over. Dr. Zachary called this Jarret's form of meditation. Jarret didn't know about that, but he knew that good scrambled eggs required constant motion.

· · · · ·

"How is Mallory doing?"

Harmon took a deep breath, and then released it. "She moved in with her father's family last week."

Brad had heard about that almost as soon as Mallory's car had left the Earling driveway and headed across town. Hawick was like any small town—run on property taxes and kept relevant by gossip. Last year's tragedy had rallied folks around the Earling family in the form of casseroles and Jell-O salads. Folks mowed the family's lawn and shoveled the driveway after the first snow. But after a proper period of respect for the family, which was about a week, kindness gave way to a telephone game of speculation and innuendo. The more benign stories dissected Jarret's failed suicide attempt and the motive behind it. The more outlandish rumors had Mallory pregnant and Jarret framed for poisoning a neighbor's dog. The Earlings hadn't escaped scrutiny either—just last week Brad had heard someone whispering that Harmon was seeing some widow behind Janet's back. It was the squicky part of small town living that fascinated Brad as much as it abhorred him.

"How are you doing with Mallory's absence?" Brad asked.

"Given things with Janet—well, and Jarret—I wonder if it's for the best. I think . . ." Harmon paused for a moment and studied the knots in the tablecloth, jaw tightening. "I think I, I mean we, did the best we could given the circumstances."

Brad ignored the undercurrent of annoyance in Harmon's voice and looked over the old man's shoulder. Pictures of better times hung on the backdrop of wallpaper sprigged with mint green flowers: a 1990s family picture of the Earlings with their only child Janice, a picture of Janice holding Mallory on her baptism day. Brad had looked at the church records last fall and had done the mental math—Brian and Janice Hartung had been married in April of 1998 and Mallory came along that August, born full-term. Brad shook his head and looked at the latest school pictures of the kids. Pictures weren't up yet for the new school year. Last year's Jarret looked almost underfed, the front of his brown hair spiked up carefully for his school picture, his pimpled chin angled just so to reduce the camera flash's glare off of his wire-rimmed glasses. Then there was Mallory; she hadn't changed much from one year to the next. However, Brad saw what Harmon was hinting at: Mallory was a dead ringer for her late mother.

Brad smelled bread toasting in the kitchen and his stomach gave a quiet growl. Harmon had asked Brad to come over at around 10:30 in the morning, and although the two men hadn't had much to say, it was close to lunchtime. Brad was about to say something when Harmon tensed. Brad heard Jarret's footfalls as the teenager lumbered from the kitchen, past them toward the three-season porch.

"Every day is a crap shoot," Harmon muttered. "I never know how either of them are. How they're going to be." Harmon didn't bother to keep his voice down, but it didn't matter—Jarret ignored them, intent on his mission to deliver a plate of eggs to his grandma.

Harmon shook his head. "Damn pills they got him on have turned his mind to mush and made him all flabby."

Brad's stomach chose that moment to let out an audible growl. "Sorry," he mumbled, and reached for one of the cookies sitting on a nearby plate.

"You might want to skip the cookies," Harmon said. He looked over to the porch, where Jarret fumbled with the patio door. Janet Earling looked fragile under her afghan, staring motionless out into the cornfield that marked the edge of town where the house was built some forty years before.

"Janet loves to freeze things. Always has, but hard to say if that was made last month, last year, or five years ago. She forgets things, you know. Makes it hard to eat unless Jarret is cooking, and all he makes are those damn scrambled eggs." Harmon retrieved a candy dish from the sideboard and handed it to Brad. It was full of the make-a-mix candy that Brad's own grandparents kept handy. "Might rot your teeth, but you won't get food poisoning."

Jarret remembered the day he looked at his reflection and saw what a growth spurt and 75 extra pounds had done. He had gone from skinny geek to the spitting image of his father. The mirror at the hospital wasn't a real mirror, it was plastic—one of those safety mirrors. Jarret stared at himself then, thinking that Dad wouldn't be able to razz him anymore about how puny he was. He'd wondered what his dad would've thought, if he wasn't a hundred miles away, both of them locked . . .

"You killed her!"

Jarret stopped short at Grandma's snarl as he walked through the patio door, one foot in the living room, one foot on the porch—the safest spot in the house to park Grandma: away from the kitchen and the knives that could cut her. Away from the gas stove she sometimes forgot to turn off. Away from the family photos that messed with her mind and let her forget that Mama was one half of a failed murder-suicide attempt.

Suicide hadn't worked for Jarret either, but at least he had tried. Dad only fired his gun once before he chickened out and tried to blame Mama's death on an intruder.

"It's Jarret, Grandma." He pitched his voice low, like he remembered the nurses doing for him on the nights he woke up to his own terrors. Some nights Jarret dreamt of the blood on the garage floor. Other nights his mind fixated on how Mama's hand seemed to be tucked under the front driver's side tire of her car. The screams that brought the nurses running were echoes of Mallory's shrieks to call 911.

He carefully set the plate of eggs on the wicker end table near Grandma Janet and stood perfectly still as her eyes raked over him. Mama had been the one who noticed that Grandma was forgetting things. Mama was the one who reminded Grandma of people's names. Grandma kept her lip curled until comprehension dawned on her face.

"Oh, Jarry," she said. "Come to see me today? Where's Mallory?" Jarret let out the breath he didn't realize he was holding.

"My boy," she said proudly. It was weird how Grandma's mind worked; angry one moment, restored to the grandma he had always adored in the next breath. She patted the couch cushion next to her, its flowers faded from several summers' worth of sunshine, and Jarret happily complied.

Jarret missed Mama. And some days he could admit that he missed his father. But both of those people were gone from his life—Grandma was still in his life, but she wasn't the person Jarret grew up with. She had stopped doing the things that he always remembered her doing: She'd quit smoking and, instead of gaining weight like Mama had, seemingly disappeared before his eyes. She had stopped coloring her hair too, Norwegian ash replacing what had once been a fine, fake mahogany.

"Who's out there with your grandpa, honey?"

"The pastor," Jarret replied.

Grandma craned her neck to look back into the dining room. "My word, that young man is going to be as bald as Grandpa before he knows it."

Jarret didn't bother to stifle his laugh. Grandma Janet joined in.

The moment was gone too soon. Just like Grandma had a radar for mess, Grandpa seemed to be the happiness police. Both Jarret and Grandma stopped laughing when Grandpa came out to the porch and cleared his throat. Grandma caught Jarret's hand in hers and gave it a squeeze.

"Pastor Brad is going to stay with you this afternoon while Grandma and I go out," Harmon finally said, frowning as he studied Jarret and Grandma's joined hands. Jarret coached himself to breathe through the disappointment he felt, running through the relaxation exercises that Dr. Zachary had taught him. Jarret knew Grandma's dementia made her act like she did, but Grandpa was harder to understand. Just two weeks ago, Grandpa had hugged him when he told him about the opening at the memory care center in Castleton. Then this morning, Grandpa was pissed off and told him that Jarret and Grandma were just costing him more money with their damn mental problems.

"It's time to go," Harmon said gruffly.

The pastor's face was pale and set as he stepped out onto the porch. Jarret didn't blame him—Grandma was smiling now, but that could change. Grandpa hadn't told her where they were going, just packed a single suitcase with some clothes and underwear.

Jarret leaned over and gave Grandma a hug, praying that he wouldn't cry. "Love you," he whispered.

Grandma's arms were bony around his shoulders. She held on tight. "Why, I love you too!"

Janet Earling hadn't taken two steps when she transitioned from loving grandma to a hellcat that had Pastor Brad in her arctic blue sights. Brad had tried to be graceful about not noticing the towel folded up underneath Janet, but the dark nap of the terry cloth and Brad's nostrils alerted him to the whiff of old urine as the lady ambled across the floor.

Janet turned to him as she passed him in the doorway. "You don't be filling my grandson's head full of any of your B.S. You hear me?" Janet Earling barely weighed 100 pounds, had a cane in one hand and the plate of eggs in her other; she shouldn't have looked formidable, but she was. Suddenly, Brad Forland understood why the Hawick County Sheriff's Department assigned extra deputies to protect Brian Hartung during the trial for his wife's murder. Minnesota didn't have the death penalty, but Janet Earling was capable enough to serve as judge, jury, and executioner. Incontinence didn't diminish this matriarch.

Brad flickered a glance over at Harmon Earling, whose own expression was barely concealed impatience. The tension that had been building that morning in Brad's gut only increased as Janet Earling toddled closer to the front door of her house.

Nothing in seminary had prepared Brad for this. He turned toward Harmon Earling and saw Janet Earling's lone suitcase waiting in the kitchen, just as its owner did.

Scrambled eggs flew as Janet whipped the Corelle plate at her husband. "You bastard!" The plate didn't break, but bong-ed and rotated on the floor between Harmon Earling and the patio door.

"I KNEW IT!" Luckily for Harmon, his wife needed her cane for balance. But Janet took after him, scooping up and flinging eggs at her husband instead of coming after him with her wood-crafted cane with a wicked looking metal handgrip. "You're going to put me in the home and shack up with that hussy Betty Bryant!"

Brushing eggs off of the front of his shirt, Harmon grabbed his wife by her spindly arm and towed her towards the door. Brad heard the anger warring with hurt in her cigarette-cracked timber. "I knew it!" Janet shrieked. "I knew it!"

Heart hammering, Brad looked up to see Jarret staring at him, the boy's dull eyes glittering with unshed tears behind the smeared lenses of his wire-rimmed glasses.

Jarret rubbed the scar on his arm as he looked at the scattered droppings of eggs on the floor. "I can make more."

SCRAMBLED EGGS

INGREDIENTS

- 2 eggs per person
- Splash of milk (amounts to about 2 tbsp. of milk for every 2 eggs; decrease the amount of milk as you increase the number of eggs used)
- Salt and pepper (optional)

DIRECTIONS

Crack the eggs into a bowl and add milk. Spray a non-stick skillet with cooking spray and set over medium-high heat. Lightly whisk the eggs and milk together. Add to heated skillet and start turning with a spatula as soon as the underside of the eggs start cooking. Keep turning the eggs until fully cooked, scraping the bottom of the pan to keep the eggs from sticking. Remove from heat, plate, and season with salt and pepper (optional).

If you are looking for an egg dish that's a little more elegant, but is easy and feeds a crowd, try this oven omelet:

GLORIA'S OVEN OMELET

Adapted from Relish (www.relish.com/recipes/southwest-oven-omelet/)

INGREDIENTS

- 1 (4 ½ oz.) can of green chilies
- 8 oz. shredded cheese*
- 1 lb. browned turkey or pork sausage
- 2 (5 oz.) cans of evaporated milk
- 8 eggs
- 2 tbsp. flour

DIRECTIONS

Preheat oven to 325 degrees. Grease or butter a baking dish (9 x 13 is the recommended size for this recipe—decrease the cooking temperature to 300 and increase the cooking time if you're using a smaller pan). Whisk together the eggs, evaporated milk, and flour in a large bowl.

Add the rest of the ingredients. Pour into prepared pan and bake for one hour, or until eggs are set in the middle and the casserole is lightly browned on top.

*The original recipe calls for Monterey Jack cheese. My family uses sharp cheddar or whatever we have on hand when we're making it. For a true southwestern flair, Mexican-blend cheeses are also a fabulous addition and can give an extra kick depending on what brand you use.

Kitchen Matters

BY LORI L. LAKE

WITH SWEAT STINGING her eyelids and hard-packed dirt against the left side of her body, Blair Brody shifted position under an enormous green tractor used for planting. Underneath, the machine resembled several entwined praying mantises. From a distance, it looked like a bug-green alien riding around on yellow tractor wheels.

She pulled on a hose attached to a crappy compressor that kept overheating and slid forward to aim at a new section of filth. Squeezing the grip of the blow gun, she aimed powerful shots of air at debris, mud, and other bits of crud. The worst part was when the dirt and chaff came back at her face or stuck in her hair.

She knew she was a sight. She was particularly pissed about that because it was Friday night, and she didn't go back to her high school until Monday. This meant she had to figure out some way to get cleaned up, since she sure as hell wasn't going to stink like fertilizer and vermin over the weekend. She supposed she'd have to wait until dark and have a spit-bath in cold water.

Blair had only realized there was a problem in the barn when she caught sight of rodents scurrying about under the tractor. They only did that when something was there to eat. She wished she'd noticed sooner. Last Monday had been unusually cloudy and overcast for late May, but her stepfather still chose to send the farm hands out into the field to begin planting soybeans. By noon, the fields were awash in rainfall. Over the next four days, Blue Earth County had received record amounts of precipitation, and in those waterlogged conditions, further planting was out. The entire acreage planted on Monday would be lost, too.

She was furious with Paulson, Becker, and Travis, the three operators responsible for the proper care of the ancient John Deere. Ever since Old Man Shepard retired, things had gone wrong on the farm. The guys knew full well that before they parked the machine, they were required to crank up the compressor and spray the tractor and seeder clean. Whoever attended to it had done a great job on the visible portions but neglected the undercarriage, which was exactly where it most needed cleaning. She had no doubt that when it was time to resume planting, those three boneheads wouldn't check the undercarriage. They'd take the tractor out with all the parts gummed up, and the finicky tractor would break down out in the field.

Despite the fact that the big green machine looked immensely powerful as it drilled and planted, it had always been prone to breakdowns and malfunctions. For the past three years, Blair had babied it as much as her late father's aging 1972 Ferrari GTC/4, which sat under a tarp in the back corner of the barn. The Ferrari was also green—but a sparkly forest green. The main difference between the two engines was that she could usually get the John Deere running, but she still had some carburetor tuning to do on the Ferrari before it would run consistently.

Blair checked again for mice. Finding no rodents, she scooted to the front of the machine and sprayed the last big chunks off the frame, then made her way around on her knees, hitting the undercarriage with shots of air whenever she noticed any other dried crud. She crawled out from beneath, rolled up the hose, and made her way over to turn off the compressor. Now she had another half hour's work ahead to rake up all the debris she'd removed.

A flood of rage coursed through her. Nobody cared about the equipment until it broke down. Then she'd get pulled out of class, off the softball field, or even out of bed in the middle of the night to haul her ass down to the equipment barn or the fields to fix problems that could have been avoided if only people followed the long-established procedures.

As of this morning, whenever a machine went haywire, Blair wouldn't have to haul her ass from anywhere but down the barn's loft ladder. Her stepfather had banned her from the house for mentioning that once she graduated from high school, she planned to join the military. He'd gone a little nutso, which was something that had been occurring far too often lately.

She had no clue why he'd ever in a million years expect her to stay out on the godforsaken farm repairing equipment and knuckling under his iron fist. It had never occurred to her that she would not—or could not—go out into the world and seek her own fortune.

"You're not leaving," he'd said earlier, menace in his voice, when she first spoke of her plans.

Blair sat across from him at the kitchen table while his newest wife, Mandy, whisked raw eggs in a bowl at the counter. Blair said, "School's out in two weeks, and I turn eighteen pretty quick after that."

"So what." He scowled. "You're staying here 'til I say different." He patted the pocket of his flannel shirt, looking for his cigarettes, but they weren't there. "You take up smoking, Blair? You got my cigs?"

"Of course not." She hated the filthy habit and the way his Marlboros made her clothes smell. She almost wished he had a pack, though, because sometimes smoking made him calmer. In a quiet, rational voice, she said, "I've thought all of this through, Ron. I'll stay long enough to make sure things are in good shape after planting, and then I'd like to take the funds you owe me and go enlist."

"That's the stupidest thing I ever heard. Are you an idiot? You're needed here, so you aren't going off and getting yourself shot up in I-raq or I-ran."

Blair had once tried to correct his pronunciation. For her trouble she'd gotten a smack upside the head and sent to her room. She squared her shoulders. "Ron, sounds like you don't want to hear this, but I'm going."

"Not gonna happen." His voice rose. "Your lazy ass will be working out in the barn, makin' sure the equipment is in good repair. You hear?"

"No, sir, I can't do that. I have plans for my life."

"Right," he said in a mocking voice.

She couldn't help but wonder why all the conflict from him originated in the kitchen. Always the kitchen. "Look, I already filled out the paperwork to join the Army. All that's left is for me to sign it when I turn eighteen."

He pushed his chair back in a rage, a long string of curse words spilling from his mouth. In his haste to rise, one thigh caught the edge of the table and lifted it a foot off the ground. The silverware clinked, and the table leg made a loud thunk when it landed. With a red face and veins popping out all over his forehead, Ron Folsham was a frightening sight.

Blair had suffered through many of his frenzied tirades over the years. When she was eleven, terror had been her only response. Now, seven years later, she'd gained eighty pounds of lean muscle and some serious athletic ability. He didn't seem afraid of her, but for the last year he'd displayed cautious restraint. He hadn't hit her for a long time. Maybe that was because of his new wife Mandy. He'd been on good behavior for their first ten months together. Lately, though, the honeymoon seemed to be over.

Blair chose not to stand up and flaunt the fact that she was nearly a head taller than his five-six height. She stayed seated and crossed her arms over her chest, waiting warily to see what would happen.

"This farm is at its limit," he hollered, his hands moving like a small windmill. "First Shep ditches me, and now I'm paying out money hand over fist, and for what! Bunch of lazy hands and bad equipment. And then there's you—you greedy ingrate."

Blair knew better than to defend herself. No matter what she said, he wouldn't hear it, but still she tried. "I'm not a kid anymore. I deserve a life. Why would I stay here with you after all you've done?"

He came toward her, shaking his index finger in her face. "All I've done? I gave you a home, food, clothes, whatever you needed for your schooling. And you pay me back by walking out? I've done everything for you."

"But you never wanted to. I was always in the way until you figured out I had mechanical skills. Now I'm your indentured servant for the rest of my life?"

"You little bitch." Hands fisted, eyes narrowed to slits, he towered over her like a volcano about to spew.

Mandy slid a plate of frittatas to the middle of the table. Blair reached for the serving fork, but before she could pick it up, her stepfather swept his arm across the tabletop. The plate and juice glasses flew across the room. They smashed into the wall and fell into piles of broken glass and yellow-and-tan curds.

Blair leapt to her feet.

Mandy whimpered and waved her hands. "Ron, Ron, please." She reached tentatively for his arm.

He shrugged her off. "You think you're so smart, Blair, so important. Well, you're not. Get out."

Blair gauged the distance between the back kitchen door and her position behind the table. She had to get past him, and that was risky. She noted that all the silverware—especially the knives—was nowhere near, so the worst he could do was strike her.

"Go on," he said in a low dangerous voice. "Get out. I know we're stuck with you 'til you graduate, but from here on out, you can sleep in the barn. Or take one of the sheds for all I care. Don't bother coming back in here for anything."

"You can't do that," Blair said as calmly as she could.

"Watch me." A nasty smile grew on his reddened face. "Call it a permanent timeout, little girl."

She gestured toward the smashed up breakfast. "What about—"

"You can forget all about eating my food in my house. If you're so damn independent and won't contribute to this family, then go feed yourself. You're not welcome in this house ever again. Get out."

He stepped back with a smirk on his face and leaned against the island kitchen counter. What other choice did she have?

She left.

Blair was hot with anger for quite some time, but eventually she knew she had to make some plans. Sleeping in the barn loft would be no great joy. She'd have to assemble a comfortable bedroll and a frame with netting to keep out the late-night bugs. She could buy a microwave at the thrift store. The old outhouse beyond the far end of the barn hadn't been used for years, but it was available. The biggest issue was that the only running water she could access outside the house was a cold faucet into a two-by-two-foot tub designed for filling buckets. She'd need to get to school early each day to use the shower facilities and stay as clean as possible over the weekends.

She grew hungrier as the day went on, and she had nothing to read. It was so wet out that she couldn't even plant anything in the vegetable garden. Her homework was on her bed inside the house.

All she could do was keep watch, and after the dinner hour, Ron finally got in his pickup and went to town. She waited to be sure he wasn't just going for cigarettes and returning right away.

After a while, she knocked at the back door. Blair had an argument carefully crafted, and if Ron's wife wouldn't allow her admittance, she might have to force her way in. But when her stepmother came to the door, Mandy burst into tears. Her shoulder-length blonde hair was loose, but didn't manage to obscure the bruise high on the cheekbone of her pretty, heart-shaped face.

"I'm so sorry, Blair. I—I—didn't know what to do this morning."

With relief, Blair said, "It's not your fault. He's just crazy and out of control. Look, I need to get clothes, school stuff, you know. From my room, I mean."

Mandy opened the door wide. "Hurry. I don't know how long he'll be gone. I hope he went to a bar, but he may just be bringing some booze home."

Weeks earlier, just in case, Blair had gathered and hidden important documents: birth certificate, social security card, school ID, and her parents' death certificates. She'd also saved over two thousand dollars. She didn't know what she would do without those funds to buy the things she needed while she stayed in the barn.

Mandy called up the stairs. "Hurry, Blair. Take the most important things that you need for now. Don't worry, I'll pack up the rest and get it to you bit by bit."

Blair surveyed the room. She didn't actually have all that much. She stuffed a bunch of clothes in a duffel bag. Her school books went into her backpack, and she got a grip on it all and clattered down the stairs to hustle into the kitchen.

Mandy said, "Take all that over to the barn, then come back. I'm putting together some sandwiches and fruit for you. I'll put some ice and water bottles in a cooler."

Blair hesitated. She was hungry, but now that she had her money, she could walk to town. "Don't get yourself in trouble. You can't afford for him to notice."

Mandy rolled her eyes. "You think he pays the slightest bit of attention to the kitchen? I could have a human head in the fridge and he'd never know."

Blair laughed. "Thank you for being so nice, Mandy. I haven't been all that kind to—"

"No, no, never mind. No need to bring up the past. Let's just make it through the coming days."

Blair thanked her and headed to the barn. The air smelled fresh, the rain had stopped, and she was controlling her destiny. But still, everything would be a lot harder now.

• • • • •

Blair got into a routine which was made much easier by the fact that she only had to survive a short while, and then her plan for enlisting would work out. So what if she exchanged one battlefield for another? At least she'd chosen the one where she could join others to contribute to the country. She felt her whole life—ever since her mother died—had been one long battle. Her father had died in a farm combine accident when she was four months old. Her mother remarried ten years later. At first Ron had been a decent stepfather, but she was glad she'd never gotten to the point of calling him Dad. It seemed like one day her mother was sick; the next she was dead of cancer, leaving Blair alone with a stepdad who lacked both compassion and self-control.

Over the years she had hoped that some other family member would pop up and help her escape the isolation of the farm, but it had never happened. Not until she was fifteen did she figure out how to use the Internet to trace her family roots. Her mother's maiden name was Johnson, the second most popular last name in the U.S. Her father's name wasn't quite as common, but there were a lot of Brodys around the country.

Blair had no credit card, so the school librarian used her own in exchange for the payment so Blair could establish an account with a genealogy search website. She learned her paternal grandparents, Mary and Alfred, were dead. Her father, Matthew MacArthur Brady, had two siblings: a sister who'd died young and a brother whom Blair had not yet located. She had hoped to find him before she joined the military, but she'd had no luck as yet.

· · · · ·

The days went by, and school finally let out. Receiving her diploma was like being issued a ticket to the Land of Oz. She knew there wouldn't be a yellow brick road, but the dirt road leading from the farm to the rest of world would do just fine.

Ron did not grace her with his presence at the graduation ceremony that sunny June afternoon, and that was just fine with her. The month before, he also hadn't shown up for—or even commented on—her qualification for the State track meet. She came in third in the 400-meter dash, and her 800-meter relay team finished first. It was too bad he couldn't be proud of her accomplishments, but it wasn't something she expected anyway.

She walked home from the after-graduation party in cool evening air filled with the sound of crickets. The same sense of opening, of blooming and expanding, was going on all around, and inside her too. She remembered this feeling from childhood, when her mother taught her how to play hopscotch and how to skip. She recalled the feeling that every wish could come true, every effort was possible. She was tempted to skip now, but she was close to home and didn't want her stepfather to see and mock her.

When she emerged from the long lane to the circular dirt area in front of the farmhouse, Ron's truck wasn't parked there. That was a relief. Last thing she needed was him making comments about her GPA again. The report card came in the mail the day before addressed to THE PARENT(S) OF. Her last term came in at a B+ and he'd gone off in a rage.

Blair headed to the kitchen door and popped open the screen. "Mandy?" she called out.

Bumping noises came from upstairs, so she figured Mandy was busy cleaning. She stepped in to wait next to the kitchen's island counter. When she heard the thumpety-thump of feet on the stairs, she opened her mouth to speak. Before she could give voice to a greeting, her stepfather came through the doorway, barefoot and wearing jeans and a dirty white T-shirt.

"What the hell are you doing in here?" he said as he strode across the kitchen floor.

With a sinking feeling, she realized he must have parked the truck on the other side of the house. She wanted to kick herself for not checking first.

He roared, "Wasn't I clear this house is off-limits?"

Before she could answer, he was upon her. She got an arm up to deflect his fist, but a second blow hit her shoulder and knocked her against the counter.

"Stop, Ron," she hollered. "Stop!"

"You little bitch."

She gauged the distance to the back door, but he was in the way.

Ron glanced at the counter and did a double-take. He grabbed at the knife block and came up with a butcher knife. Flipping it in his hand, the blade ended up pointing down. He held it in what looked to Blair like a death-grip.

She was already moving to the other end of the counter. Would she be able to keep the island between herself and him until he calmed down? She smelled the pungent aroma of alcohol. *Oh, no,* she thought. *Not again.*

His face was flushed dark red, his hair in disarray. He looked like he'd already been in a fight—that he'd won. And now he was ready to win again.

Wheezing like an angry bull, he said, "You been nothin' but a misery for all these years. First, I lost your mother. Then Sharon went 'cause of you. And now probably Mandy, too." With the back of his shirt sleeve he wiped beads of sweat off his forehead.

Without warning, he dodged around the side of the counter and came at her.

Blair jumped to other side of the counter, ready to keep moving whenever he did. He was still in the way of the back door, and she didn't think she could make it through the hall, living room, and foyer to get the front door open. Even drunk, he was too fast.

"You have to calm down, Ron. You're—"

"Don't you tell me what to do. Screw you and the pooch you rode in on."

The comment was so ludicrous that Blair would have laughed if she didn't feel her life was in danger. Instead she said, "What do you want from me? I told you I can stay until planting is done."

"Only planting gonna be done is your body out in the east acres."

Was he serious? She couldn't tell if it was the booze speaking or if all his real intentions were coming out because the alcohol had loosened his tongue.

He came at her again. This time he got around the counter just fast enough to take a swipe at her with the knife. The blade caught the back of her upper arm but it didn't hurt, so she figured it was only a scrape.

Moving faster than she ever had on a running track, she dove toward the back door. He still managed to smack into her, and she went down.

In an instant, she popped back up.

He raised the knife over his head and lunged.

As if in slow motion, she brought her leg up in a side kick and nailed him in the lower abdomen.

He staggered back, fell. His head hit the edge of the counter with a crunching sound.

He went down like a sack of wet dirt.

Hands fisted as she crouched low, Blair saw the knife's trajectory as it left his hand and tumbled end over end. It hit the wall, rebounded, and came to rest against a table leg.

She looked down at Ron, expecting him to rise up like an inflatable pop-up clown punching bag. Instead, she couldn't even hear him breathing. He lay on the floor, one eye closed, the other at half mast. A puddle of red slowly gathered under his head, spreading fast like oil leaking from a punctured oil pan.

Blair's whole body felt numb. If he got up now, she didn't know if she could move. A motion, a blur on her left, and suddenly Mandy stood in the kitchen doorway, her lip split, face red, all the buttons on the front of her blouse torn off.

"Run," Mandy said. "Run!"

"What about you?"

"I'll deal with it, Blair. Just get out of here."

"But what if—"

"Go!" Mandy screamed.

On shaky legs, Blair crashed through the screen door, knocking it hard against the side of the house. At the barn, she clambered up to the loft, grabbed a box and her coat in one arm, and nearly fell as she navigated back down the ladder. From the coat pocket she took out keys as she hastened to cross the barn's dirt floor. She pulled the tarp off the old Ferrari and unlocked the trunk. She'd already stashed most of the things she was taking with her, but she added the box and jacket and slammed the lid shut.

She scrambled into the driver's seat. *Please God,* she thought, *please let the car start.* It took three tries, but on the third, the engine turned over. She thought she'd pee her pants in relief. Shifting into reverse, she threw her arm along the top of the passenger seat to look over her shoulder. As the car rolled back toward the wide slider door, she realized her light blue oxford shirt didn't look right. How had she gotten it so dirty?

Once she'd backed out of the barn, she hit the brakes, jammed the car into drive, and released the clutch. The Ferrari took off like a rocket toward the long lane leaving the farm. She quickly shifted gears as the engine roared in approval.

She was safe. She was away from that maniac. He wouldn't come after her again.

She choked for air. *Oh my God, oh my God, I killed Ron.* Her breath came in short gasps. Her whole body still felt fired up, as though red-hot lava flowed in her veins, but very quickly the heat dissipated. Shivering, she turned onto the main road that led to town, slowed, and left the car in third gear. She needed to take stock. What should she do? Go back? Go to the police station? Run to Canada? She shut her eyes for a brief moment, then focused on the road again. Oh, no. She'd killed her stepfather—the military was never going to let her enlist.

Hot tears of fear and anger coursed down her cheeks. She raised her left arm to wipe them away and noticed that her sleeve was stained black. What the heck? Just like that, her triceps burned like a fire poker was scorching to the back of her arm. She tried to examine the injury but couldn't see it in the darkness.

With a cry of frustration, Blair pulled off to the side of the road and leaned her head against the steering wheel. After a few moments, she turned the key, and the engine gurgled to halt.

The nighttime critters were silent. The only sound she heard was the engine cooling, tick-tick-tick-tick . . . the sound of a clock running out during her last moments of freedom. How long would it take the police to track the flashy green Ferrari? Where could she stay—and for how long—with the ID of someone named Blair Brody? Too bad she hadn't been named Mary Johnson, after her paternal grandmother. How would she work, what life could she have?

She had to face the situation. She knew that now. Running away had been the wrong decision.

She pushed in the clutch and turned the key. The engine wanted to turn over.

C'mon, baby, please start, she thought.

She tried to be careful not to flood it, but she must have. The Ferrari refused to cooperate. She felt lightheaded with exasperation. And fatigue. She'd never felt so tired in her life.

Half a mile beyond, where the road arced south, headlights appeared. Three sets of them came around the bend and straightened out. As the vehicles drew closer, the lights blinded Blair. She squinted her eyelids shut, heard a whoosh as one car went by, then another whoosh. When she opened her eyes, the third car was slowing. A police cruiser crawled along past, turned around, and parked behind her. Flashing red and blue and white lights glared into her mirrors, and she could see nothing until a beefy officer came alongside the car and shone his flashlight inside. He was a big guy wearing dark pants, a light shirt, and a patrol jacket. She rolled down the window and tried to focus.

"Miss?"

When she heard his voice, Blair opened her mouth but she couldn't make any words come out. She had no idea what to say anyway.

"Miss, do you have something to do with what's going on up at the farm?"

She nodded. A sense of vertigo swept through her, as if she were sliding off the deck of a very big ship.

"Miss, could you step out of the car? Miss?"

She realized she'd never put on her seatbelt. She was a murderer and a seatbelt offender. Would they care about that if they got her on the murder charge?

Feeling like she was being cast about in deep water, she pulled at the door handle. Why did it seem that it was taking all her strength to push open the car door?

As she swung her feet out of the car, white dots swirled around in her vision. "Snowing?" she mumbled.

"What?" The big man settled his hat on his head and eased forward. "Are you okay, Miss?"

"No. I . . . guess . . . not."

Blair was dreaming of a long road stretched far out in the distance. The world around her was pitch-dark, so she wasn't sure why she could see the ribbon of road so clearly.

Someone spoke, but she couldn't understand his words. She felt pressure on her eyelids. Glaring light blinded her, the brightest headlights she'd ever seen. Something was preventing her from moving her head. She struggled. A voice said, "It's okay. You're safe. Just relax for a while and we'll fix you right up."

The road went dark, and Blair went with it.

Blair came to full consciousness slowly, as if she were an hourglass with sand slowly filtering from the top to the bottom. She lay on her right side, her left arm pinned against her chest. For a moment, she thought that when she opened her eyes, the old John Deere seeder would be above her, waiting for a good cleaning. But she recognized she wasn't in the barn. Nothing smelled right. Too sharp and medicinal, like latex gloves and iodine and strong soap. She could only conclude that she was in the hospital.

Sunlight streamed into the room, and opening her eyes didn't seem like a good idea. She wanted to move, but something was blocking her so she couldn't roll flat on her back. In front of her, pillows were tucked under her abdomen and thighs. She felt as confined as a pig in a tiny pen.

"You need to stay on your side," a woman's voice said.

Blair blinked and yawned. Her vision focused, and she noticed that a tube was taped to the back of her hand. Blair looked at it in wonder. She'd never had an IV line before.

"What's . . . happening?" She squinted. Her vision cleared a little, and she saw Mandy sitting in a chair next to the bed.

"What are you . . . doing here?" As Blair spoke, she noticed Mandy had two black eyes, a butterfly bandage on her cheekbone, and what appeared to be stitches in her lower lip.

Mandy rose and came to the side of the bed. "I wanted to make sure you were okay."

"What happened . . . to you?"

"Don't you remember Ron attacking you last night?"

The events in the kitchen came rushing in so fast, Blair felt like a powerful vise had grabbed hold of her lungs and squeezed. She breathed hard to catch her breath. "Is he alive? Did I kill him?"

Mandy put a hand gently on Blair's forehead. "Unfortunately, the man will live."

"What do you mean—unfortunately?"

"He's been drunk so often lately. Unless he stops that, he doesn't deserve a good life. I'm leaving him, Blair. I thought the first beating was an anomaly, and I forgave him. Then a couple months ago, he did it again. I almost left then, but I wanted to watch out for you until you could get away safely. Then he beat me last night, and that was it. I'm done."

"You stayed to look out for me?"

Mandy stroked Blair's dark hair. "Yes, especially after the shenanigans with him throwing you out of the house. That was ridiculously cruel. He doesn't have the right to do that."

"I'm sorry I left you, Mandy. I shouldn't have run away."

"I told you to go. It was fine. I just didn't realize he'd stabbed you. If I had—"

"My arm." Blair remembered the dark stains on the sleeve of her blouse. "He cut me. I thought he'd missed."

"Yeah, adrenaline does that to a person. You could have bled to death. The doctor said something about a brachial artery being partly severed and some other veins cut in the back of your arm. You lost a lot of blood. That's why you need to stay still. The doctors did surgery to repair the blood vessels. You're just lucky the county cop found you in time."

A deep voice boomed from the doorway. "Speaking of county cops, is it okay if one comes in to visit?"

"Sure." Mandy said as she moved away from the bed. "I'll step out and get a cup of coffee so you two can talk."

Blair was sorry Mandy had removed her warm hand from her brow. The touch had been reassuring. Now this cop was probably showing up to handcuff her to the bedrail. The officer came around the foot of the bed and stood so Blair could see him.

She gazed up into his wide face. "I remember you. Sort of."

"Uh huh. You fell into my arms like a tall, hulking sack a' taters." He laughed, which sounded to Blair like a grunting woodchuck. "Glad I could get you to the hospital in time."

"What's going to happen to me?"

"Well, kid, you'll heal up. Don't worry about that."

"That's not what I mean. I thought I killed my stepfather. Aren't you going to take my statement and put me in lockup?"

"Oh, no. Your stepmom saw everything that happened. The city cops will get a statement from you soon enough. That's not my job. But we've got Mrs. Folsham's report and all the physical evidence at the scene. Clearly self-defense all the way. You're in the clear, kid."

Blair blinked back tears. "I won't be charged at all?"

"Nope." The officer moved closer and bent a little so he could speak softly. He leaned in enough that she could read the gold nametag on his uniform: *Norbert*. Officer Norbert. There were some kids at her school with that last name.

"Miss Brody," he said softly, "I can tell you right now, you have me on your side. No offense, but your stepfather was a bastard. I remember playing football with him in high school. He was a year behind me. See this?" He held his hand up to show Blair a faint pattern dotted on his palm. "He wore illegal metal spikes on his football shoes. We were both receivers my junior year, and he wanted first string, but I'd earned it fair and square. One day in practice I got tackled, and while I was down, he ran over and stomped on my palm. On purpose. Broke three bones and punctured me like a pin cushion. Put me out injured for more than half the season. All these years later, my palm still aches when it rains."

Officer Norbert stepped back, lowered himself into the chair, and laced his fingers together over his ample belly. "A man don't forget that kind of unnecessary, mean-spirited behavior. I always suspected that self-serving bastard Ronnie Folsham wasn't ever gonna grow out of that behavior, and I was right. I'm just surprised it's took him so long to wind up in jail."

"He's going to jail?"

"Oh, he's going to prison. He stabbed you. Attempted murder won't be easy to get out of even if he was drunk. The beatings that Mrs. Folsham will testify about will get him for domestic abuse, too. I'd say he'll go away for several years. You can take over your farm and do what you want now."

He rose and clamped his hat on his big head. "Gotta run."

"Wait. What's this about the farm?"

"That's your farm, young lady. The Brody homestead. I remember your dad. I knew him in grade school. We went to different high schools though. He was a good guy. Left that farm to you."

"Ron said my dad left it to my mom, and when she died, it became his."

"That lyin' sack of sh—whoops! I should watch my mouth." He made that woodchuck gargling sound again. "Miss Brody, the farm is yours to work, sell, rent out, whatever you want. Once you get out of the hospital, I'm sure it'll all come together." He strode toward the door. "You'll heal fast, so don't worry. Let me know if you have any questions. I gave my card to your stepmom."

When he left, he took the air and noise right out of the room, leaving only the tiny blipping sound of the IV dripping fluid into her veins.

Blair lay there for a while, contemplating this new piece of information. She owned the farm? Now it made sense that he'd never spoken much about the farm, and he sure didn't want anyone asking questions about it.

She couldn't get over his audacity—or her own amazement. She owned a farm! She had options. And people on her side. And she'd be eighteen in a few days. With any luck at all, she might not ever have to see Ron again.

Her stomach grumbled. When was the last time she'd eaten? She couldn't remember. What she wouldn't give for one of Mandy's ham and egg sandwiches. Or a loaded baked potato grown in her own vegetable garden. Even better, a cheesy onion-and-bacon frittata. Her mouth watered.

She smiled and closed her eyes.

Best of all, she thought, *I own a Ferrari.*

LORI'S CRIMINALLY TASTY FRITTATA RECIPE

INGREDIENTS

The base
- 4 large eggs, 5 medium eggs, or 6 dinky eggs
- ¼ cup liquid (broth, V8 juice, tomato juice, etc.)
- ¼ tsp. of spice/herbs (i.e. dried thyme leaves; chopped fresh herbs such as chives, basil, dill, parsley, or cilantro; powdered oregano, onion salt, or garlic salt—the key is to pick spice[s] that go with your filling [below])
- Salt and pepper (to your own personal taste—you can always add S&P at the table)

The filling
- 1 cup of pre-cooked filling(s) that are cut small and drained well (beans, rice, grains, broccoli, peppers, baby corn, sugar snap peas, carrots, onions, zucchini, squash, asparagus, scallions, cherry tomatoes, spinach, avocado, pasta bits, potato chunks, shrimp or other seafood, salmon, bacon, sausage, chicken chunks, and various cheeses—almost anything goes, even leftovers)
- 3 tsp. olive oil, butter, or vegetable oil. (match your oil with your fillings so things taste integrated—i.e. spicy V8 with onions, bell pepper, zucchini, and basil might taste best with olive oil; milk, potato chunks, broccoli, and scallions might call for butter)

DIRECTIONS

Beat your base (the first four ingredients) in a medium bowl with a lead pipe or big spoon until blended. Do not overbeat the mixture. Set aside. Add your filling (the second set of ingredients) to the bowl containing your base. Mix well with a large knife or billy club. Heat butter/oil until melted in an 8-inch "bakeable" frying pan or cast iron skillet using a medium-hot blowtorch burner. Pour entire mixture into skillet on medium heat. Stir until eggs thicken and scream and start to pull away from the edges of the pan. Remove skillet from stove top and transfer entire pan to a 350° oven. Keep an eye on it for 12 to 16 minutes until eggs are completely set without any liquid remaining. To serve, slide frittata onto a platter face-up OR flip it upside down onto a platter to show the browned bottom OR just put the skillet on the table and use a killing knife to cut wedges right out of the pan. Serves 4 to 6, depending on starvation level.

Sweet Justice

BY BRIAN LUTTERMAN

THE DEFENDANT WAS going down fast, but not without a fight. "I wasn't there," insisted Lanny McKelvey, a bald, scholarly-looking guy who sat rigidly on the witness stand.

I was in full prosecutorial mode—indignant and incredulous. "What about the three witnesses who saw you at the Burger King that day?" I demanded. "The ones who saw you take the envelope from Mr. Greene?"

He managed a weak smile. "They're mistaken, I'm afraid."

I looked over at the jury and could see they weren't buying it. We had introduced exterior surveillance footage that showed another man, Ronald Greene, driving up to the restaurant in his distinctive white Cadillac. But we'd needed human eyewitnesses from inside the building to prove that Greene had handed Lanny McKelvey an envelope containing a $10,000 bribe. All three witnesses had been firm in their testimony. After that, FBI agent John Gibson had taken the stand, using bank records to trace the influx of the money into McKelvey's accounts. McKelvey, with no real defense, had decided to simply hunker down, deny everything, and make us prove our case. It was the legal version of the rope-a-dope.

Ronald Greene would stand trial when we'd finished with McKelvey, and I wondered what strategy he would employ. He didn't appear to be a genius; he'd handed the bribe openly across the table to McKelvey in full view of multiple witnesses, who had actually seen money sticking out of the envelope. In another bad decision, Greene had turned down my offer of leniency in exchange for his testimony against McKelvey.

As a prosecutor, I needed to make defendants seem unlikable to a jury of average citizens. But Lanny McKelvey, besides being crooked, was an IRS agent. I've had tougher tasks.

"What about the ruling you issued in favor of Mr. Greene's company two weeks after the exchange at the restaurant?" I asked.

"I was simply following the law," McKelvey insisted.

"You reversed yourself after that exchange," I countered, brandishing a letter, previously introduced into evidence, in which he had initially denied Greene's request for a favorable interpretation of the tax code. "Your reversal saved Mr. Greene a ton of money."

"Objection," said the defense attorney, a woman who looked about nineteen. "Is there a question here?"

The judge peered down at me over half-glasses. I wondered if judges were automatically issued half-glasses, along with their gavels and robes. US District Judge Raymond T. Cooley was a cranky old fart who'd insisted on holding court today, on Christmas Eve. *Humbug.* "Ms. Wilkinson?"

I threw up my hands. "I withdraw the question, Your Honor."

"But there was no question," the teenage defense attorney whined.

"We know what she means," the judge snapped. To me: "Move along."

"No further questions," I said.

The witness was excused. The judge called the defense counsel and me up to the bench and grudgingly allowed that it was Christmas Eve, and even though it was only 2:00 pm, we would now adjourn for the holiday weekend. He released the jury, and we were all free to go.

Finally, I thought. Like everybody, I was anxious to get home. But there was a task to be completed first. I closed up the file box containing our exhibits, pulled a Tupperware container out of my briefcase, and set out in my wheelchair for the judge's chambers, in the hallway behind the courtroom.

A young clerk named Diane was chatting with the bailiff as she put papers into a drawer.

She looked up when I rolled in. "Hey, Pen."

"Merry Christmas, Diane." I held out the plastic container. I always try to take care of the court staff at holiday time.

She glanced into the box. "Ooh—looks good." She took the proffered confectionary treat and was about to bite into it, but was stopped by a voice from the doorway.

"Don't," said FBI Special Agent John Gibson.

"Why not?" Diane asked.

"Those are Mounds bars."

"Like the candy bars?"

"Better," Gibson said. "A lot better. Don't fall into the trap."

"What trap?" asked the bailiff, a chunky guy named Judd, who walked over toward Diane's desk.

"Just don't get started on the Mounds bars," the FBI agent warned.

"To heck with that," said Diane, and bit into the bar. Her face morphed into a mask of wonderment. "My God, what on earth is this?"

"My Grandma Doris's recipe," I replied, as she completed the remainder of the bar in two bites. I held up the box to Judd, who gave Gibson an uneasy look as he bit into his serving.

"Holy cow," the bailiff said. "Was your grandmother a witch or something? How do you make this stuff?"

"Well, dark chocolate and coconut, obviously," Diane guessed. "You can bet there's a ton of sugar."

"Let's hear it for sugar," Judd muttered. "Next guy who pleads the Twinkie defense walks."

"Let's clear out, people," boomed a voice from the door. The Honorable Raymond T. Cooley strode past Gibson into the room, stopped at the door to his private chambers, and glanced around, as if noticing us for the first time. I held out the plastic container. "Have a Mounds bar, Judge."

The judge took the last one from the box and snarfed it. His face remained blank for a long moment before showing astonishment. "Forget the defendant. You should be the one charged with bribing a public official, Ms. Wilkinson."

"Sorry, Your Honor."

Cooley reached into the box for a second bar but came up empty. He looked at me, alarmed.

"I—um, don't have any more," I said. I didn't tell him Gibson had eaten most of my supply at lunchtime.

The judge glared at me for a long moment, probably considering whether to hold me in contempt. Finally he turned on his heel and disappeared into his office.

"Merry Christmas," I said to the slammed door.

I turned to Diane and Judd, who stared at me in anger and disbelief.

"Told you it was a trap," Gibson said.

"Merry Christmas," I said, and rolled quickly to the courtroom.

"That went well," Gibson said in the hallway as he walked ahead of me, opening doors. "You managed to alienate both the judge and his staff."

"A special talent of mine."

"They were fools, thinking they could just sample those bars. They're like crack."

"It's Christmas and we're winning the case, John. A little more positivity would be in order." We gathered up my exhibits and notes, which Gibson helped carry.

"Plans tonight, Pen?" he asked as we boarded the elevator, taking us up to my office in the Federal courthouse in downtown Los Angeles.

"My sister is in town. She lives in Tampa, and her son is flying in this afternoon."

"How about James?"

"In Minnesota." My boyfriend, James Carter, had gone to Minneapolis to spend the holiday with his daughter. "We're cooking a nice turkey dinner tonight."

"With Mounds bars for dessert?"

"Of course. I made a double batch. What are you doing?"

"Family stuff at home. In-laws. The usual. Helping my wife with the cooking."

I was glad I had help with the cooking, too. Even in younger days, before the accident that had left me a paraplegic, I hadn't been much of a culinary artist. But when it came to Grandma Doris's Mounds bars, I was Michelangelo.

Fighting through miserable traffic on the I-710, I made my way home to Long Beach. As I pulled into my driveway, my sister, Marsha, called me from LAX airport to say she had picked up her son and they were on their way.

"Good," I said. "I'll get things started here. Eleanor volunteered to help." My landlady, Eleanor Tompkins, lived in the upstairs unit of my duplex. She was a widow, and we'd invited her to join us for dinner.

"See you soon," Marsha said. "And don't touch the Mounds bars."

• • • • •

A light was on in my apartment as I pulled into the driveway. I wasn't surprised; Eleanor had a key and had promised to check on the turkey a couple of times during the day. I opened the door on my handicapped van, extended the ramp, and rolled out. Then I closed up the van, rolled up the ramp leading to my door, and inserted my key into the lock. The door was already open. "Eleanor?"

She didn't answer. I struggled out of my coat, draped it over a chair, and went into the kitchen. I didn't see anything right away, but then I nearly ran over something on the floor.

A body.

I looked down and gave a little shriek. Eleanor Tompkins lay face down on the floor, motionless. There was a little pool of blood next to her face. I leaned down and was able to touch her shoulder. She was breathing.

I shook her gently. "Eleanor?" No response. On the floor nearby, I saw my rolling pin, speckled with blood. The injury hadn't been an accident.

I pulled out my phone and called 911, asking for the police as well as an ambulance. Then I called Marsha. "How far away are you?" I asked when she answered.

"Maybe five minutes."

"Hurry. Eleanor is hurt. It may be serious." While I waited, I retrieved a first-aid kit I kept in the bathroom, found a big gauze pad, and managed to lean down and reach the wound on Eleanor's head. I glanced around the kitchen; the oven door was open, and the turkey was out on the counter. I closed the oven door and waited.

Marsha arrived first, rushing in with her teenage son, Kenny, in tow. She crouched down, inspected the wound with her practiced nurse's eye, and wrapped tape around Eleanor's head to secure the gauze. Then she gently turned the older woman over. "Eleanor?" The victim stirred a little and moaned.

The ambulance arrived. As the paramedics loaded Eleanor onto a stretcher, I asked Marsha to go to the hospital with her. I'd have to stay and deal with the police. As they left, I called John Gibson and explained what had happened. He said he'd be right down, but since he lived at the other end of the city, in the San Fernando Valley, it would probably take at least an hour. I looked quickly around the apartment and found nothing missing.

The police showed up a few minutes later. Two youngish male officers asked a few quick questions, then went through the neighborhood, looking for witnesses. After they'd left, I turned to Kenny. "You thought you were in for a boring holiday with boring relatives."

"It's sure not boring," he said, looking appalled and excited at the same time.

While the officers were canvassing the neighborhood, a police fingerprint guy checked out the doorknob, rolling pin, and a few other surfaces. "Once we eliminate your prints, I doubt there will be anything here we can use," he reported.

The police officers returned. "Nobody saw an assailant enter the unit," a freckled, redheaded cop reported. "No vehicles in the driveway, either, although the perp could have parked on the street."

"I checked with the hospital," said the other cop, a tall, languid guy. "The victim is conscious, but doesn't remember anything about the attack. She's got a concussion."

"Damn," I said, disappointed but relieved that Eleanor was apparently going to be okay. I felt a surge of anger at the unknown creep who had attacked a kindly old lady. The officers took my statement, thanked me, and said they would run their report by the detectives after the holiday.

John Gibson arrived as the cops were leaving and briefly conferred with them outside before coming in. I introduced him to Kenny, and Gibson looked over the crime scene in the kitchen before sitting with me in the living room. Kenny made himself useful by cleaning up the kitchen floor.

"What do you think happened?" Gibson asked.

"The door was unlocked. Eleanor was just going to do a quick check on the turkey and probably didn't relock it. It looks like the assailant sneaked up behind her, since she was hit on the back of the head and fell forward. But we may never know for sure, unless Eleanor regains her memory."

"The big question is motive," Gibson said. "They didn't take anything. They must have been watching her, and when they saw her come down to your unit and leave the door unlocked, they took the opportunity."

"But what if they weren't watching Eleanor?"

He gave me a puzzled look. "What do you mean?"

"What if they were watching my apartment? Waiting for me?"

"You mean you may have been the intended target?"

"Well . . ."

"You've got a point, Pen. In fact, what's wrong with that theory?"

"Other than Eleanor being twice my age, a hundred pounds heavier, Filipina, and able to walk, nothing. The guy would have to be an idiot, John. Besides, who would want to attack me?"

Even as the words left my mouth, I thought of several people who wouldn't mind giving me a whack on the head. But none of them would mistake Eleanor for me.

"What if it had something to do with the trial?" he said.

"It's not unthinkable. If I was killed or incapacitated during the trial . . ."

"There'd be a mistrial. Then we'd have to re-try McKelvey, who now knows our strategy and our weaknesses. He'd love another crack at us. The trouble is, he knows what you look like."

"But what about his accomplice? Ronald Greene has never met me in person."

"You said only an idiot would mistake Eleanor for you."

"That would be Greene."

Gibson called the Long Beach Police and persuaded them to check the neighborhood again, this time asking specifically about Greene, whose picture they would obtain from the FBI.

I was listening to the conversation. "Don't forget to check for his white Cadillac," I said.

"Right," Gibson said into the phone. "Run down his vehicle as well."

"There's something else they should look for," said a voice from across the room. We turned and looked at Kenny, who was holding up a nine-by-thirteen pan of Mounds bars. A large block was missing from one corner.

"And have them look for chocolate," Gibson said into the phone. There was further discussion, which ended with Gibson saying, "Yes, chocolate, damnit." He clicked off the phone.

An hour later, we were all gathered around Eleanor's bedside at the hospital. Eleanor, thankfully, was awake and talking, although she was still groggy from the painkiller and the blow to the head.

Gibson's phone buzzed, and he stepped out onto the corridor to take the call. He returned a few minutes later. "Got him," the FBI agent reported. "Two witnesses saw Greene's car in the neighborhood, so the cops went to question him. Turns out he lives nearby. He stonewalled at first, but then one of the cops spotted chocolate on his shirt and a pant leg. When they confronted him with that, he spilled everything. Admitted to the attack on Eleanor and said McKelvey had put him up to it. They've arrested him."

"Thank God," Eleanor exclaimed.

I sighed. "The turkey is ruined. I'm afraid we won't have quite the celebration we'd planned for tonight."

"It's not so bad," Kenny said. "There are plenty of Mounds bars left."

"You're right," Marsha said. "The ultimate holiday treat."

"And crime-fighting tool," I added.

MOUNDS BARS

INGREDIENTS

- 2 cups crushed graham crackers
- ½ cup sugar
- ½ cup butter
- 2 cups flaked coconut
- 1 can sweetened condensed milk
- 1 12-oz. package chocolate chips
- 2 tbsp. peanut butter

DIRECTIONS

Mix crackers, sugar, and butter. Pat into bottom of 9 x 13 pan. On top, pour sweetened condensed milk and coconut. Bake 15 minutes at 350 degrees. Melt chocolate chips and peanut butter together and spread on cooled bars.

Cupcake Battle Royale

BY BRIAN LANDON

LUCILLE WARWICK WASN'T going to lose. She couldn't lose. After all, she was the best baker in the Midwest. This was the competition she was made for. This was her town. And by God, these were her cupcakes.

A local television program, *Minnesota Today*, was hosting a competition similar to a popular television game show that featured established bakers facing off in challenges that require creativity, technique, and a mastery of baking.

Lucille wasn't a contestant by chance. The show's host, Ted Stanley, was a regular customer at her shop Cup o' Love. He'd whispered to her that not only should she apply to be on the show, but she had the best chance of winning. Since it was music to her ears, she sent Mr. Stanley away with a box of her best assortment of cupcakes and a promise that she would submit her application that evening. She heard back almost immediately.

Now that she had arrived in the studio, it all seemed so much more real. More intense. As the two other bakers arrived—a young woman, no more than twenty years old, and a middle-aged, pale, vegan-looking fellow—her confidence bloomed. Not only did she want to take them down. No, she wanted to conquer them. She could cut the tension between the three of them with a rubber spatula.

It wasn't all ego, however. Lucille was also intrigued by the $30,000 grant provided by Minnesota's historic Gold Medal Flour Company. Her store was her pride and joy, and her cupcakes were phenomenal . . . but finances were not in her skill set. She needed that money to keep her business on the rise, so to speak. She needed it badly.

The middle-aged man, who was unnaturally skinny—especially for a

52

baker—had a dopey grin on his face. What was he smiling about? Didn't he know what he was in for? It made Lucille unsettled. Did he actually think he could beat her?

Not wanting to get distracted, Lucille decided to return her attention to her assigned table and her bevy of ingredients that were provided for her. She wanted to memorize each jar, each container, so that when she needed something, there would be no panicked searching. Just confident, swift action.

She observed the fresh cherries, strawberries, and blueberries at her table. She tasted them. Sweet. Delicious. Perfect. Lucille had told Mr. Stanley that fresh fruit was her secret ingredient. Maybe he'd decided to tilt things in her favor? To her surprise, she too had a dopey grin on her face.

The lights turned on one by one as the crew funneled into the studio to begin their day of work. All three contestants had shown up early hoping to get a leg up on the competition. Tony recognized an older, middle-aged woman from a shop in town. She looked confident. He couldn't relate.

Tony Dunphy, amateur baker and recovering drug addict, was nervous. Okay, nervous wasn't the right word. He was downright petrified. Recovering was also not the right word. As of five minutes ago, he was very actively using drugs in a feeble attempt to calm his nerves. It was backfiring in spectacular fashion.

The host, Ted Stanley, had discovered him at the local Salvation Army center. He said he needed an inspirational story to be part of his annual Cupcake Battle Royale program on *Minnesota Today*. Tony knew how to bake a little—he'd watched his mother bake when he was a kid, prior to her bout with cancer. But what he lacked in culinary talent, he made up for in greed for the prize money. He really, really wanted it. He could live on his own. Pay rent. Pay off his numerous debtors. Perhaps buy some high-quality merchandise . . .

Tony just hoped he could hold off the shakes until after the conclusion of the program. As Ted Stanley made his entrance onto the set, Tony could feel his heart rate increase, his brow sweat, and his fingers start to twitch.

He is far more handsome in person, thought Melissa as Ted Stanley adjusted his tie in front of a camera monitor. Not that she was attracted to him. She was just attracted to his career.

Since Melissa had graduated from culinary school, she had hoped to land a hosting job on the Food Network. Maybe her own show—*Meals by Melissa* had a nice ring to it. Until then, she was willing to take any cooking-themed gig that came along. When Ted Stanley had an open casting call at her school, he'd said that her talent was exactly the kind he was looking for.

Melissa would be the first to admit that it wasn't her cooking talent that got her onto the show. After all, she had zero cooking skills. Nada. Bupkiss. She once tried cooking turkey tetrazzini and wound up with a malodorous turkey loaf. It was not good.

But Ted Stanley seemed to find her attractive. And maybe . . . just maybe, it could be all she needed to win the competition.

"Bakers—the competition is about to begin!" announced Ted Stanley, directing the cameras to each of the three contestants. "Once again, your first challenge is to design cupcakes that perfectly represent our great state of Minnesota. Your challenge begins . . ." Stanley paused for dramatic effect. "NOW!"

Immediately, Lucille got to work on her trademark cupcake—the Spoon and Cherry cupcake, modeled after the infamous statue featured at the Walker Art Center. It was a vanilla cupcake with a cherry gel center, topped with a fondant spoon and cherry. It was such a wonderful design, it genuinely bothered people to eat the cupcake and destroy the artistry.

While Lucille whisked together the flour, milk, sugar, and eggs, she glanced up at her competition. Melissa was relentlessly flirting with Ted

Stanley. She wasn't even looking at what she was doing. Sugar? Salt? That blonde dunderhead probably had no idea what she was dumping into her mixing bowl. But Ted Stanley was laughing and reciprocating. Was she actually in danger of losing a competition to this . . . this . . . kitchen hussy?

Then Lucille noticed her other competitor—the scrawny, sickly-looking fellow. He was shaking like a leaf. He was trying to crack eggs, but his hand kept missing the edge of the bowl and instead he kept smashing eggs right into the table.

No competition there, thought Lucille. I've got this in the bag.

Ted Stanley smiled and welcomed the audience back from commercial break. "Judges, what did you think of our Minnesota-themed cupcakes from round one?"

One of the two judges, a silver-haired local news anchor, said, "Lucille—your 'Cherry and Spoon' was absolutely delightful. Perfectly pillowy cake topped with an intricate design that really appealed to the eyes."

Lucille smiled. Excellent, she thought. The others are toast.

The other judge, a young, spry weather man from the same network, said, "Melissa—your loon-inspired marble cupcakes were delicious and elegant in their simplicity. In fact, I'd say they're good enough to be the official State Cupcake."

Both judges and Ted Stanley broke into horribly fake TV laughter. *Yuck it up, chuckleheads*, thought Lucille.

The silver-haired anchor turned his attention to Tony, who was squinting as he looked at them. "Tony—your cupcakes . . . well, they never quite got finished, and I'm not so sure you knew what you were doing."

Lucille glanced over at Tony. He was standing upright, but his gaze seemed to be focused on the corner of the room rather than the judge who was talking to him. Was he falling asleep? A small torrent of drool fell out of his mouth.

Ted Stanley looked intently at the two judges. "Do we have a decision?"

The weatherman looked as pained to bring bad news to the cupcake contestants as he usually was to report rain on the weekend. "Tony, I'm sorry—but you will not be moving on in this competition."

At that very moment, Tony's eyes went wide and he face-planted on the floor. The studio went very quiet.

Lucille was shocked by what had happened, but she was even more shocked when she caught a glimpse of Melissa. She had a distinct smile on her face. Lucille knew that smile well. She had it all the time herself. It's the smile that said, No one can stop me.

Then Melissa turned and looked at Lucille directly. She winked.

For the first time, Lucille was scared.

Melissa tried her best to smile and send positive thoughts to the other . . . err, living contestant, and the judges. She winked at Lucille as if to say, *Nothing to worry about. Everything is okay!*

Unfortunately, Melissa had realized a little too late that doing a line of coke with Tony before the show was a mistake. They had gotten to the studio around the same time, and he seemed so withdrawn and sluggish. Having worked in a few kitchens, Melissa knew that sometimes you needed a little pick-me-up to get through a busy day. She honestly thought she was offering a helping hand. It may or may not have led to his death—but that was for the coroner to decide later. Either way, it was an accident and something no one needed to know she was connected with. She would just keep on smiling.

For now, she had a competition to think about. Although to be honest, she really didn't care about winning or losing anymore. She just wanted to go home and have a glass of wine.

Ted Stanley, with a somber expression that looked just as false as his positive expression, said to the camera, "Ladies and gentleman, we have unfortunately lost one of our contestants due to what we can only assume is an unknown medical condition. That being said, we will continue with our competition and the final round between Lucille Warwick and Melissa Davis."

Lucille and Melissa nodded that they were ready to continue.

"For the final round, there will be no themes. Lucille and Melissa each need to make their very best cupcake. No rules. No gimmicks. Just the most delicious and beautiful cupcake they can create."

Melissa looked at Lucille and shrugged. This seemed pretty straightforward. She didn't know if she'd win or not, but at least it wouldn't take too much brain power. She'd just make her chocolate molten raspberry lava cupcakes, which seemed to be her only culinary creation that her family and friends could keep down. That would be her best chance at winning.

"But there will be a catch," said Ted Stanley. "Unfortunately, I can't tell you quite yet. You will begin . . . NOW."

The time clock started. They were being given an hour and fifteen minutes to complete their very best cupcakes. For Melissa, this meant chopping the fresh raspberries and letting them sit in a simple syrup while she stirred her chocolate batter together.

The problem was that Melissa was severely allergic to raspberries, so she had to be careful with how she handled them. She put latex gloves on her hands and proceeded to carefully chop the raspberries.

Melissa glanced up to see what Lucille was doing for her cupcakes, but when she did, Melissa cut into an especially juicy raspberry. A couple rivulets of juice splashed onto her neck. It itched horribly. She whipped off a glove and rubbed a finger across her neck.

Melissa glanced back at Lucille. She had a strange look on her face.

That's it, thought Lucille. *I can't believe she's openly threatening me in front of a live studio audience.* Lucille watched as Melissa slid a finger across her neck as if to say, *"I'm going to kill you, Lucille. I'm going to kill you because I want to win."*

If that's the way she wants to play it, thought Lucille, *then so be it.*

When Lucille's mother Beatrice first opened Cup o' Love back in the early eighties, she'd had significant obstacles to overcome, including several competing neighborhood bakeries, financial difficulties, and worse of all, her savage bastard of a husband. The only reason why Cup o' Love survived—and perhaps the reason why Beatrice and Lucille survived—was because Beatrice had taken extra steps to ensure their survival. Steps that Beatrice had shared with her daughter in confidence several years after the premature death of her husband, Lucille's father.

Lucille never shamed her mother or scorned her for what she did. When Beatrice passed a few years back, Lucille gladly accepted the bakery that she inherited. It came with an understanding—that desperate times call for desperate measures. And perhaps more importantly—never take shit from anyone.

Lucille looked around her. The studio audience had mostly dissipated for the time being. No one wanted to wait around for seventy-five minutes to watch people bake. Lucille assumed some clever editing would be done to ensure it appeared as though a completely enthralled audience was watching for the duration.

Lucille bit her lip. She casually reached into her pocket and palmed a small vial. She walked directly to Melissa's table.

"How are your cupcakes coming along?" asked Lucille, with an over-the-top friendliness to her voice.

"Okay, but I accidentally got a little juice—"

"Say, is that some confectioner's sugar you got down there?" Lucille was pointing at a shelf of supplies underneath the baker's table.

"Umm . . . yeah, I think so," said Melissa. "Do you need some?"

"Would you mind?"

"Anything for a fellow baker," said Melissa.

Nice, thought Lucille. *The bitch is laying it on real thick.*

As Melissa reached below her table, Lucille emptied the contents of the vial into Melissa's molten chocolate batter.

It was enough arsenic to kill a small army.

Melissa stood back up and handed the bag of sugar to Lucille. "Just bring back whatever you don't use."

"Of course, dear," said Lucille with a devilish grin.

To her own surprise, a tear drop fell down Lucille's face. She realized she'd never felt so close to her mother until this very moment.

"Bakers!" announced Ted Stanley. "It is time for the catch! Not only must you must make enough for our judges, but also enough for everyone in this studio, including our fabulous audience!" This was inevitably followed by thunderous applause.

Lucille raised her eyebrow, an inkling of real concern clawing at her conscience.

"Can you believe this?" asked Melissa. "I'll have to multiply everything by twenty. Shoot."

Lucille swallowed. She looked around at the dozens of people in the audience. Old women. Moms. A couple of young children. Families.

"Umm—maybe, maybe we should just dump out what we got and start from scratch," said Lucille.

Melissa shook her head. "We only have so much for ingredients. I can't spare a thing. Can I get the rest of that confectioner's sugar? Looks like you got a whole bag right there."

Lucille's brow became moist. "Yeah, sure." She picked up the bag and handed it to Melissa.

Not knowing what else to do, Lucille began haphazardly tossing ingredients into her own mixing bowl and expanding her recipe to accommodate several dozen people. She watched as Melissa dumped candied raspberries into her batter.

"Melissa," said Lucille. "Maybe you should try out your batter before you try to make so many."

Melissa shook her head. "I know this recipe like the back of my hand. Besides, I can't eat it. I'm allergic to raspberries."

Shit, shit, shit, thought Lucille.

"Throw it away," said Lucille. "All of it."

Melissa furrowed her brow. "No," she said. "Just worry about your own cupcakes and I'll worry about mine, okay?"

Lucille softly growled.

"Unless you don't think you can win?" asked Melissa with a playful smile.

Bad move, bitch, thought Lucille.

Lucille had to admit, Melissa was doing an admirable job of expanding the volume of the batter. There would definitely be enough for everyone in the studio.

As the buzzer sounded, several assistants entered the studio to take the cupcakes and distribute them to the judges and the studio audience.

Lucille watched with great interest.

Ted Stanley flashed his pearly whites and said, "Lucille, tell us about your cupcakes."

"Well," said Lucille, "I made a marble cupcake using dark chocolate, cocoa butter, and fresh vanilla bean mascarpone. It's topped with a light hazelnut cream cheese frosting."

The judges praised her work. "Incredible," one said. "Best I've ever had," said the other. The studio audience seemed more than pleased with her offering.

Lucille grinned from ear to ear.

"Melissa, tell us about your cupcake," said Ted Stanley.

"Everyone in my family loves this cupcake and says it's their absolute favorite. It's a molten chocolate raspberry cupcake with powdered sugar and whipped cream on top."

"And you, yourself, are allergic to raspberries, is that right?"

Melissa nodded. "I can't even touch it without breaking out. Today, for example, I got a few drops on my neck and now I'm itching like crazy."

Oh, thought Lucille. *So she wasn't threatening me. Whoops-a-daisy.*

One judge took a giant bite and said, "Are you telling me that you were not able to taste the cupcakes you made?"

"Right," said Melissa. "I've made it so many times that it doesn't matter. I've got the recipe memorized."

"I hate to tell you this," said the judge, grimacing, "but something went wrong. There is a horribly bitter, nutty flavor. It tastes—spoiled. Bad. What did you do to this?"

The other judge took a couple bites, then spit his out. "Terrible . . ." he said as he rolled out of his chair and hit the floor.

What began as mutterings of disgust in the audience grew into rampant commotion as people jetted towards the exits, began convulsing in the aisles, vomited where they sat.

Melissa was in shock. Tears streamed down her face. "Was it really that bad?" She wasn't asking anyone in particular. Besides, only a few people in the studio were still conscious: Lucille, Ted Stanley, and Melissa. Everyone else was on the floor convulsing, dead, or in the process of dying.

"What . . . umm . . ." mumbled Ted Stanley as he tried to make sense of what happened.

"I'll take the prize money now, Ted," said Lucille, taking a bite of her own marble cupcake and savoring the smooth, creamy, non-toxic flavor of the cream cheese frosting. "It's pretty obvious who the winner is."

Melissa looked at Lucille with horror.

Lucille shrugged. "My cupcakes don't kill people."

"You," said Ted Stanley, eyeing Lucille suspiciously, "you . . . poisoned everyone?"

Lucille shook her head. "If prissy girl wasn't afraid of a fucking raspberry, everyone in this studio audience would be alive right now. This is all your fault, you know."

Melissa wailed as she ran to the exit.

"You're insane," said Ted Stanley. "You know this is all on camera, right?"

Lucille perked up. She had completely forgotten.

Ted Stanley shook his head as he followed Melissa to the exit, tripping over a couple bodies as he did so.

Lucille stared into the camera. Her eyes were as wide as her smile.

"I won," she said. "I won the cupcake battle!"

Lucille exhaled a sigh of contentment. She held onto her metal whisk as if it were a bouquet of roses. A single teardrop rolled down her cheek.

"I dedicate this to my mother. She taught me everything I know."

RASPBERRY ARSENIC SWIRL CUPCAKES

INGREDIENTS

Cupcakes
- 1½ cups sifted all-purpose flour
- ⅜ tsp. baking soda
- ¾ tsp. cream of tartar
- ½ tsp. salt
- 1 cup granulated sugar
- ½ cup unsalted butter at room temperature
- 6 tbsp. mayonnaise
- 1 tsp. vanilla extract
- ½ tsp. almond extract
- ½ cup unsweetened vanilla almond milk
- 1 jar raspberry pie filling
- Arsenic (optional)

Frosting
- 1 cup shortening
- 4 cups powdered sugar
- 2 tbsp. unsweetened vanilla almond milk
- 1 tsp. vanilla extract
- ¾ tsp. almond extract

DIRECTIONS

Preheat oven to 350 degrees and line a cupcake pan with 12 liners. In a bowl, whisk together the flour, baking soda, cream of tartar, and salt. In a separate bowl or stand mixer, beat the sugar, butter, and mayonnaise together until creamy. Stir in vanilla and almond extracts. Add the flour mixture and milk alternately, starting and ending with the flour and mix until all of the flour is incorporated. Do not beat or overmix. Divide the batter evenly into the 12 cupcake liners. Add 1 tsp. of the syrup from the pie filling (avoid the raspberries—you will use these to top the cupcake) to each cup and use a toothpick to swirl it into the batter. Bake for about 25 minutes or until a toothpick inserted into the center comes out clean.

While the cupcakes are cooking, make the frosting by beating the shortening until creamy. Then add one cup of powdered sugar at a time, beating on low after each addition. Once all of the powdered sugar is added, add the milk and extracts and beat until smooth. Once the cupcakes are cool, frost them and top each one with a raspberry from the jar of pie filling.

Blueberry Bliss

BY CATHLENE N. BUCHHOLZ

I GUESS YOU could say I was suffering from pastry on the brain when I discovered the woman's battered body lying face down in the parking lot of Patty-Lou's Pie Shop. My first thought was, *Gee, this is sure to create quite the stir at the annual pie toss contest.* My second thought was, *What the heck was I thinking, showing up early for work just to get a jumpstart on the coffee crowd?* But apparently my co-worker Lizzy must have had the same idea. Her brown Buick, with a bumper sticker that read: *Will Work for Dough*, sat in the dark morning shadows next to the back entry door.

I had pulled my rusty Toyota pick-up into its usual spot alongside the dumpster, and that's when I saw the shoe. I wondered if Lizzy had decided to forego her footwear, as she often threatened to do. I climbed out of the truck and peeked around the large metal container prepared to see its match. Instead, my eyes found a wooden rolling pin covered with flour, blood, and perhaps a wee bit of brain tissue resting next to a woman's bare right foot.

Despite the change of clothes from waitress garb to after-hours frump-wear, Lizzy wore her 200 pounds lying down as well as she did standing up. Her sassy, red-dyed hair appeared matted with blood, yet the majority of the strands held their curl quite nicely around her neck and ears. I dared not turn her over; surely her eyelids would pop open and she'd grab me. Instead, I did what any well-meaning citizen would do: I backtracked to the safety of my car to mull over the situation.

If I'd had a lick of common sense, I would've hightailed it out of the parking lot and gone back home to crawl under the covers for another good hour. But I was young, stupid, and scared. My mind scrambled across town to an image of Sheriff Al Warren—big and beefy, but with hands that could calm a skittish hen. Then a picture of Deputy Steve Lawson shot to the forefront of my brain. Short, wiry, and clean-shaven, the kid was barely twenty and fresh out of the Twin Cities' Police Academy. Most of the locals, *moi* included, referred to the sheriff's sidekick as Stevie. Not in front of the sheriff, of course. That man had one helluva temper and wasn't afraid to show it. I plucked my cell phone out of my purse, prayed for both a strong signal and the sheriff's voice, and punched in 911.

Stevie arrived precisely six minutes later, lights flashing. I led him around to the back of the shop to Lizzy's body. It was still dark out, almost five a.m., and the single light in the small gravel parking lot barely reached the tree line next to the dumpster. With a trembling hand, I motioned to the blood-splattered rolling pin that lay on the ground.

First thing Stevie did was take a few stumbling steps forward, squat down, and feel for a pulse. "Damn!" He punched a button on his walkie-talkie, his hand shaking. "This is Deputy Lawson. Please respond." Phone static crackled and popped in return. "I repeat, this is Deputy Lawson. Do I got myself a 10-4?" Stevie glanced nervously at me and then darted upright, fumbling for his newly-issued Smith & Wesson. "We need to secure the area," he whispered more to himself than to me. "This looks like a crime scene."

I wanted to say, "*Well, duh, Einstein. Ya think?*" But another glance at Lizzy's dead body reeled me in and reminded me to keep my trap shut.

Ears cocked, he swept his revolver left and right. His eyes squinted toward the trees and then back to me. "Listen, now, Charlotte. That's your name, right?"

I nodded.

"I want you to go on back into the shop and put a call in for Sheriff Warren. Use the landline." He holstered his gun and squared his shoulders. "Don't let Betty give you any lip. You say that Deputy Lawson requests that the sheriff be woken up. I want him out here ASAP."

The back entry door to the pie shop was ajar and, with a quick glance back at Stevie, who was busy slapping his walkie-talkie against his thigh, I turned to enter. After flipping on the main lights, I noted several pies knocked to the floor. Dark, lumpy filling was splattered here and there—Patty-Lou's Blueberry Bliss, no doubt. Lizzy's matching shoe rested under a prep table. My pulse quickened. I tiptoed to the double swinging doors. "Anybody here?" I squeaked, pushing them open. As I slipped through, my mind slid back in time to my first visit to the restaurant.

It had been a hot and humid Minnesota morning, and I was on college break—home to earn some jingle. Aunt Rita was the one who prompted my ass to apply at one of Mille Lacs Lake's finest tourist traps—a well-known pie and coffee dive near the south shore.

"The owner, Patty-Lou, had quite the scare awhile back, what with her bad heart and all," Aunt Rita said. "Says she could use an extra hand this summer. 'Course I offered up yours."

Before I could say yea or nay, I found my butt sitting across from Patty-Lou and my head bobbing up and down.

"I need a fast-paced waitress to work the breakfast and noon hours," she said. "Hate to admit it, but this 70-year-old ticker just ain't ticking the way it's supposed to. And tourist season ain't no time to be dragging one's bunions."

After pumping my hand, Patty-Lou gave me a tour of the fifties-themed shop. The tablecloths boasted red and white checkers. A jukebox sat in the corner; Fats Domino belted out "Blueberry Hill." High red-cushioned stools with shapely chrome legs lined up next to the breakfast bar. I caught a glimpse of my dazed expression in a large mirror that acted as a backdrop behind the percolating coffee machines and spotted glassware. A banner strung on the wall read: *Patty-Lou's Pies! Best Pies in the Midwest!* I followed Patty-Lou, the squeak of my athletic shoes drowned out by the din of customers' voices and the Big Bopper.

"And this here's the kitchen." Patty-Lou pushed through a pair of swinging doors. "It's where all that heavenly goodness is made, courtesy of sisters Doris and Dottie."

Two white-haired ladies stood by a set of large convection ovens, mitts in the air, and peered at me. "Hmf," one said, turning to open an oven door.

Patty-Lou winked at me. "Hard workers. I swear these two must hold the world's record in mass pie production. Lucky for me." She led me back out of the kitchen. "The girls start around five, but no worries. I won't need you until six." She nodded toward a middle-aged woman dressed in a waitress uniform, slouching next to a corner booth. "That's my Lizzy." Patty-Lou smiled. "Couldn't run this place without her." She leaned close to my ear. "She's had a hard life—what with that no-good-husband of hers. 'Course she won't divorce the sonuva—" She sighed. "Anyway, you could say I sorta adopted her over the years . . ."

With the memory of Lizzy, I pulled myself back to the present. *Call Sheriff Warren*, I reminded myself. As I dialed, I spied the open cash register drawer. "Oh, crap."

"I'll remind you, young lady, that we don't use that kind of language in the dining area," came a remark from behind me.

"And what kind of nonsense is going on in here, anyway?" piped a second voice.

Doris and Dottie stood in the kitchen doorway, frowning; one had the remains of a pie in her hands, and the other held up Lizzy's shoe.

Swallowing hard, I turned and pressed my ear to the receiver. "Yes . . . no . . . I don't know," I replied to Betty's slew of questions.

The two women edged closer, exchanging glances.

After Betty dispatched the sheriff, she told me to hang up but remain close to the phone. "Sheriff Warren won't want any suspects or witnesses wandering off."

Suspects? I believed in the old adage of innocent until proven guilty. Yet here was a word unspoken in my world rolling casually off Betty's tongue. Apparently certain minds thought alike—the two sisters jumped the gun and had me tried, convicted, and placed on death row by the time Sheriff Warren pulled up in his sparkle-clean county cruiser.

"Just look at her, Sheriff. It's written all over her face," Doris clucked, waggling a bony finger in my direction.

Her sister Dottie nodded, her gray curls bouncing up and down. "She was the first one here this morning."

"Which was very unusual," Doris added.

"Yes, unusual," Dottie echoed.

I glared at the two women. "Is it a crime to show up early for work?"

"Tsk, tsk," they said.

Sheriff Warren gave a long sigh and folded his meaty arms across his chest. "Hold on, now, ladies. Let's not shoot the messenger. Charlotte here did the right thing and called the police. What with the cash register tampered with and signs of a scuffle in the kitchen—"

"But Sheriff," Doris interrupted.

"But nothing. Let me remind you," Sheriff Warren continued, "that Ed Soderstrom is out back right now working on time of death. It's not official that poor little, ahem, poor Lizzy expired—"

"Was killed," Doris said.

Dottie's palm slapped the counter. "Murdered."

Sheriff Warren held up his hand as he cleared his throat. "Let Ed do his work. Deputy Lawson is canvassing the scene for clues. If I were to make an educated guess, I'd say this was an interrupted robbery gone bad." He reached for the doorknob then said over his shoulder, "Give me a shout when Patty-Lou arrives. And ladies?"

"Yes, Sheriff?" the two old ladies said in unison.

"Make sure the breakfast crowd stays put in here when word about Lizzy spreads. I don't want any rubberneckers wandering out back to muck up my scene."

I caught Patty-Lou as she walked in the door and helped her over to the prep table. She slumped onto the stool, one hand pressed to her chest, the other gripping a wet hanky. Doris and Dottie hurried over, each placing a hand on Patty-Lou's shoulders. "I can't believe it," Patty-Lou sniffled. "Still can't. Even after Sheriff Warren showed me . . . had me look at . . . I mean, what kind of hooligan breaks into an old lady's pie shop and then beats an innocent waitress to death? With a rolling pin, no less."

"It's a shame about Lizzy," Dottie said, "but—"

Doris glanced at her sister and shook her head fervently.

"You'd think that, well . . ." Patty-Lou continued, "that the person must've been desperate. And for what? A couple bucks from the till? A few fresh pies?"

"Best pies in the Midwest!" I restrained myself from saying as I peered out the back window. The sun was slowly rising, and I watched as the sheriff and deputy loaded Lizzy's body bag into the back of a van marked Mille Lacs County Coroner. Stevie was at the foot, his deputy cap askew, staggering beneath the weight.

Patty-Lou turned toward me. "Is Stevie still out there with his junior detective kit?"

"Yep. But looks like he and the sheriff are, uh, finishing up."

"Shoot. I just remembered something that might stir the sheriff's brain."

"Hold that thought," I said, still peeking out the window. "They're heading this way."

As the two men swaggered through the back door, the front door jingled, announcing the first day's customer. "Patty-Lou hoo!" a sing-song voice called out.

"Aw, nuts," Patty-Lou said. "It's Mavis from the bait shop. I don't have time for her yappity-yap right now." She looked at me. "Charlotte, will you be a sweet pea and pour her a cup of Joe?"

"Make it two cups," the sheriff said as he and Stevie joined us. "I don't need Mavis Marley in the midst of a police investigation."

After sliding the first cup of fresh brew across the counter to Mavis and serving up a warm slice of Bada Bing Cherry pie, I scurried back to the kitchen. I didn't need Doris and Dottie spinning more yarns about me being a killer and thief to the local law. To my surprise, the two old biddies had positioned themselves at another table—within hearing distance, of course—and were rolling out dough and mixing up pie filling.

The sheriff had his back to them and was leaning on the table, his large frame planted precariously on a small wooden stool, his head cocked toward Patty-Lou. Stevie stood behind him, furiously scratching notes with a stubby No. 2 pencil.

"And you say you wrote your last will and testament, when?" he was asking Patty-Lou as he held up a multi-page document.

"Well, I drove this old body over to the bank and had the latest version notarized as soon as I jumped ship out of that blasted hospital. Darn doctor acted as if I was on my deathbed."

Sheriff Warren chuckled. "Well, thank God you're not. Who'd fill our stomachs with all those famous Patty-Lou pies?"

A tin pan slipped out of Dottie's hands and clattered to the floor. Stevie dropped his pencil and paper and spun around, reaching for his holster. Dottie scrunched up her shoulders and said meekly, "Sorry."

The sheriff glared at Stevie. "Deputy Lawson? Why don't you go on out front and hobnob with the customers?" He turned back to Patty-Lou. "Now where were we?"

Patty-Lou leaned in closer and whispered, "I was thinking that maybe that fool of a husband might've done Lizzy in."

Sheriff Warren narrowed his brow. "Aw, come on now, Patty-Lou. Everyone knows Carl tends to tip the bottle a bit too much. But he seems harmless. And what does that have to do with your will?"

"That's just it," she replied. "It's in the will . . . I mean, Lizzy's in the will." She lowered her voice again. "She was set to inherit half the business if my heart ever went kerplunk for good."

The sheriff straightened in his chair and rubbed his unshaved face. "Well, this definitely cuts a chunk in my theory. Guess I'll be having a talk with a certain someone."

"Uh, Sheriff?" I timidly raised my hand. "What about the pie tossing contest?"

He stood and said in a booming voice, "No tossing anything at anybody until I get to the bottom of this."

As he hollered for Stevie, I heard Patty-Lou mutter, "Great balls of batter. It's enough to give an old woman a coronary."

Doris and Dottie looked at each other with raised eyebrows.

It was mid-morning when Stevie came flying back into the parking lot in his cruiser. He stumbled through the front door, his right hand by his waist, and called out for Patty-Lou. "She's in the back," I said. Several customers frowned, shook their heads, and then resumed eating. I made a sweep of the dining area, refilled a couple coffees, and then bee-lined it for the kitchen.

"Sheriff Warren says Carl was away on business," Stevie was reading from his notepad. "Just got back after taking the red-eye flight. And he wasn't too keen on being questioned. Especially as to his whereabouts."

Patty-Lou rolled her eyes.

"Said he heard the news about Lizzy first thing from Mavis. And although he and Lizzy were separated, he said, 'a man has a right to mourn his wife in peace.'"

"Mourn, my bum," Patty-Lou replied. "That's a crock of cow dung. That man hasn't cared a bag of beans about Lizzy since she took the highroad. Only cares about his someday inheritance from her ma and pa. And from me, if you haven't heard the word."

Stevie straightened his cap. "Well, the sheriff did find out some interesting news when he searched Lizzy's apartment." He gave a little cough and looked around. "Of course, this is just between you all and me." Doris and Dottie, who had been shuffling pies in and out of the oven, stopped, shook off their mitts, and took a step closer to us. "There was a message on her answering machine from Dottie. Time showed eleven p.m. last night." He looked at Dottie, who was fiddling with her apron, and raised his eyebrows.

"I was worried about the oven," Dottie blurted out. "I thought I had left it on. I, I couldn't sleep and was hoping Lizzy could bop on in and check, as she lives so close and all."

Doris nodded. "Lizzy does live the closest."

"I had been so busy yesterday with those Blueberry Bliss pies. Isn't that right, sister?"

"Of course, right," Doris said. "They're the favorite pick of the pies to toss."

"And eat." Dottie smiled.

Stevie cleared his throat. "Well, I guess the sheriff has it in his head that he may want to have a chat with you, Dottie."

Dottie gasped. "Me? But—"

Doris grabbed her hand. "Nothing to worry about, dear."

"First, the sheriff has to run some evidence over to the lab, and then meet with the coroner and a detective from the county."

"A detective?" Patty-Lou said. "About time they took notice."

"Sheriff Warren will swing by bright and early tomorrow. In the meantime, if there's anything you all need, just let me know." Stevie hitched up his pants and then tipped his cap. "Ladies."

I hurried after Stevie. Tugging on his sleeve, I asked, "What's this about evidence? Is it a clue to the killer? Do the rest of us need to worry when we clock out?"

Stevie smiled and patted me on the shoulder. "No need to worry. You just leave the police work to us professionals."

"Professionals," I muttered under my breath as I watched Stevie shake a few limp hands on his way out. I rushed over to the corner booth to take an order, and then turned around at the sound of laughter from the table by the picture window. Stevie's cruiser had bumped up against one of the trees that lined the parking lot. He glanced toward the restaurant, slammed the car into reverse, and then spun out of the lot.

Mavis Marley scurried in only moments later and plopped down at the breakfast bar. She waved me over. "Charlotte, honey? You have time for a break?"

I glanced around the restaurant. *Better now than never,* I thought.

In a loud stage whisper, she said, "I'm not one to spread rumors . . ."

Oh, boy, I thought. *Here we go.*

"But I heard it through the grapevine that Dottie is going to be hauled in for questioning." Mavis sighed, then shook her head. "Can't say I'm surprised, though, considering what my two eyes saw last night."

I dropped my rag on the counter. "What do you mean?" I said in a low voice. "What exactly did you see?"

"Well," she paused, fidgeting with a napkin holder, "I guess I didn't think it was too important at the time. Just a little strange, if you will."

"Yes, yes," I nodded, glancing at the clock.

"It was late, probably around midnight. I was up using the facilities. You know I have a weak bladder. Never can make it through the night without—"

"Mavis," I said, "I hate to sound rude, but I only have a few minutes. Can we make this quick?"

She frowned. "Anyway, when I glanced out the bedroom window, I do that on occasion—this town may be small, but I swear we have our share of Peeping Toms—I happened to see Dottie bicycling on past. I thought it odd, quite late for a bike ride, especially for an elderly lady like Dottie. When I called out her name, she didn't even glance in my direction. Now that was rude."

"Uh-huh."

"I suppose I should have mentioned it to the sheriff but, well, a person doesn't like to get too involved in another's business."

As I opened my mouth to respond, I felt a sharp poke in the back. Doris stood behind me, hands covered in flour, brows furrowed. "Patty-Lou says she needs you in the kitchen."

"Oh, okay. I was just taking a quick break with—"

"No problem," Mavis said. She slipped down from her stool. "We were just commiserating about Lizzy." Her eyes slid toward Doris. "Such a shame. Don't you think?"

"Yes," Doris replied. "Quite."

The soles of my feet throbbed from all the extra hours I had worked, and I was just about to pack it in for the night when my cell phone rang. It was Doris and Dottie's landline. *What the heck?* I thought as I lifted it to my ear. Dottie's shaky voice was on the other end. "Doris wants to meet you at the shop. She says it's important."

"Dottie," I said, a hint of irritation lining my speech, "Do you realize what time it is? What can be so dreadfully important that it can't wait until tomorrow morning?"

"Doris didn't, well, she didn't say exactly. Something about the pie toss and, and Patty-Lou, and, um, maybe that new pie recipe we've been working on, and, uh—"

"Okay, okay. Tell her I'm on my way. Just give me a few minutes."

By the time I pulled into the back parking lot, the dashboard clock read eleven p.m. I climbed out of my truck and glanced over at the dumpster. Yellow caution tape was still draped around the crime scene. A shiver ran down my back. Only twenty-four hours before and Lizzy had been walking, talking, and breathing.

As I headed over to the back entry door, I noticed a bicycle propped up against the wall of the restaurant. I shook my head. I could only hope that in my later years I would be in as good a shape as those two sisters.

The door was unlocked, yet the restaurant was dark. A little voice in my head said *Déjà vu*.

"Hello?" I called out. No answer. My heart began to race as I flipped the lights. *Would the killer dare to—?* My thought was interrupted by the sight of Doris as she pushed through the swinging kitchen doors. "Oh, my God," I said, letting loose my breath. "For a minute I thought that maybe . . ." I gave a small laugh. "Uh, never mind."

Doris stepped closer, holding several papers in her hand.

I took a deep breath to calm myself. "Dottie said that you needed to see me. What in the world is so important?"

"I think you already know," Doris said, slapping the papers down on the prep table. "In fact, I think you've known from the start."

"What are you talking about?"

"Trying to weasel your way into the will, just like that fast-talking, woe-is-me poster woman from Overeater's Anonymous. Every week she had some sob story. The tears, the crying, the sniffling. Patty-Lou just soaked it up."

75

My pulse began to race. "Lizzy? Is this about Lizzy?"

Doris pounded her hand on the table. "Of course, Lizzy. And then she made up some fairy-tale about that poor husband of hers, what's-his-name, Carl. Claimed spousal abuse. But I'll tell you, little Missy, we never saw a scratch on her. Leeching off that hard-working man, taking him for everything he had, but not giving him the dignity of a divorce. No wonder it drove the man to drink."

I took a step backward. Wherever this conversation was going, I didn't want to be around at the finish line.

"Dottie and I were set to inherit the place, the restaurant, the recipes, the whole shebang. At least until that woman came along and Patty-Lou got it into her noggin to change everything after the heart attack. Thought Lizzy deserved half. Half, she told us! Do you realize how that feels? Putting in hours and hours of work all these years? Trying recipes until we hit on the perfect combination of ingredients? Dottie and I came up with those famous fillings. No one else. Not Patty-Lou. Not Lizzy. And certainly not you." She shoved her sleeves up in anger, revealing several bruises and scratches on her forearms. Her hands balled into fists. "Now you tell me, where's the fairness in that?"

"Doris," I said in a low whisper, my legs trembling, my teeth beginning to chatter, "you didn't, I mean, you—"

"Did I kill her?" She threw her head back with a deep throaty cackle. "Ask Mavis Marley. She seems to know everything." She reached beneath the prep table and then withdrew a large, shiny knife. "All I can say is that woman deserved to die."

My brain said *Go* and I spun around and sprinted for the door, but Doris was surprisingly light on her feet. She grabbed a handful of my shirt and yanked me off balance. As we both fell down in a heap, the sharp sting of a blade grazed my waist. "No!" I screamed, twisting away.

I scrambled to regain my footing, losing a sneaker in the process. As my eyes darted to my feet, I couldn't help but think, *One shoe on, one shoe off*. I hobbled through the door, the safety of my truck only yards away.

A high-pitched voice stopped me in my tracks. "Police! Drop your weapon!" Stevie stepped out of the darkness. His revolver pointed slightly above and beyond my right shoulder. "I don't want to have to say it again!" The way his hands shook, I thought, *You go ahead and say it as many times as you please. Just let me ease on out of the way before you decide to pull that trigger.*

Luckily for all parties involved, the knife thudded to the ground. "Damn rookie," Doris muttered, raising her hands in the air.

I called Betty on the landline as Stevie cuffed Doris and parked her butt in the back of the squad car. By the time I moseyed out to the parking lot, my heartbeat had returned to normal. I took a deep breath and eased it out, then walked over to the car where Stevie was scribbling notes.

"What made you come back here?" I asked, waving my hand toward the dumpster.

He paused, his pencil in the air. "In the movies, the killer always returns to the scene of the crime."

I nodded.

"Besides," he added, "Dottie called. Said she was worried about her sister."

"Huh." I peered at Doris through the window. "Thank God for sisterly love, eh?"

Stevie chuckled.

"I owe you a big thank-you, Deputy Lawson."

"Steve," he said with a smile.

BLUEBERRY BLISS PIE

Courtesy of Randall Ferguson, owner/baker at randypiemn.com

Pie making is like a comforting grandmother or a pair of elastic waist pants . . . very forgiving. Consider this recipe a guide; use your gut and intuition to alter the ingredients or give it your own signature touch.

INGREDIENTS

Crust

- 2 ¼ cups flour
- 2 tbsp. sugar (plus additional for sprinkling)
- 1 tsp. salt
- 2 sticks unsalted butter (very chilled)
- 1 tbsp. vinegar
- 6 tsp. water (on the rocks)
- 1 egg white
- 1 tsp. milk

Filling

- 5-6 cups blueberries (fresh and/or frozen, try a combination of wild and domestic)
- 1 lemon
- ¾-1 cup sugar
- 6 tbsp. tapioca flour
- 4 tbsp. butter

INSTRUCTIONS

For Crust

Combine dry ingredients. Cut butter into tablespoons and mix in with pastry cutter or by hand. Mix dough until butter has become small pea-sized pieces. Add vinegar and water 1 tbsp. at a time until dough is slightly crumbly and holds together. Knead gently until smooth. Divide dough into two balls, flatten each slightly, wrap in plastic wrap. Let dough rest for 20-30 minutes before rolling out.

For Filling

Mix blueberries with zest of lemon plus juice of half the lemon. Add sugar and tapioca flour. Combine until well mixed.

Assembly

Preheat oven to 450 degrees. Roll out first disc on lightly floured surface, starting from center and rolling outward until about ⅛ inch thick. Fold dough in half and gently place onto 9-inch pie plate. Unroll, press into pie plate, and trim so there is ½-inch overhang. Pour in the filling and place 4 cut tbsp. of butter on berries.

Roll out second disc and place crust on top of pie. Trim the crust to the same size as bottom. Pressing both crusts together, roll the edges under. Either crimp crust with fingers or, using tongs of a fork, press along the edge to seal the crust from leaking. Create slits with sharp knife for air vents. Mix 1 tsp. of milk with an egg white. Use a pastry brush, lightly coat entire crust with mixture. Sprinkle additional sugar on top.

Bake

Place a large cookie sheet on lower rack (in case of leaking). Put pie into oven on middle rack. Cook for 15 minutes at 450 degrees. Place pie shield on pie, lower temperature to 375 degrees, and cook for another 35-45 minutes until crust is nicely browned and juices are bubbling thickly. Let cool for at least 2 hours before eating.

Serving Up a Surprise

BY MARLENE CHABOT

"THEY POISONED HIM, they did," Charlie Sassafrass screamed, pressing his arthritic knees deeper into the newly spread cedar mulch at the base of a wild rose bush, one of many forming the six-foot-high hedge between the length of his yard and the neighbor's.

The jarring noise gripped still-half-asleep, five-foot-two Gertie Nash, a woman in her mid-fifties, dressed in a garishly designed nightie, bathrobe, and slippers that barely covered her heavily tattooed body, as she set her brother's Schnoodle, a Schnauzer-Poodle mix, on the overly grown grass to do his dirty duty. If someone had seen Gertie out on the lawn that morning, they would've sworn she almost did a somersault as she twisted to see who dared intrude on her early morning routine before having her first cup of mocha flavored java. "What on earth—?"

Movement along the ground by the hedges separating the two yards quickly drew her attention. She caught sight of filthy hands clawing the dry earth at the base of one of the wild rose bushes. Not sure what to do, she remained where she stood and silently continued to observe the action of the hands.

It was the second dose of "They poisoned him," even louder than the first, that finally pressed the woman into action. Before her two hundred pounds of flesh waddled over to the bushes to study the person on the ground, though, she fluffed the back of her flame-red and black, shoulder-length hair. No matter what the emergency, she always liked to look her personal best. One never knew when one might bump into a newscaster filming something for the ten o'clock news deadline.

Huffing and puffing, the determined woman eventually arrived at her destination and instantly recognized the slim male figure on the ground.

"Who got poisoned, Charlie?" she calmly managed to ask.

When the seventy-five-year-old man didn't respond, Gertie decided to stroll over to his yard and find out what the problem was. But before she could lift her short legs, thick as an elephant's, off the ground, she heard Charlie's back screen door slam. *Good, one of his twin nephews who live with him must've come outside,* she thought. *They'll know what to do.*

"Uncle Charlie," a much younger kindly voice said, "what did I tell you about digging up the yard? You're going to destroy these hedges Jute and I have lovingly pampered. Now go inside and get cleaned up. Breakfast is waiting."

Nosy Gertie teetered on her tiptoes, hoping to find an opening in the hedge so she could greet Jasper, the older of the twins, before he went in. When she finally found a spot, she poked her round head through. "Oh, yoo-hoo, Jasper. Over here."

Jasper Sassafrass, impeccably dressed in a dark blue two-piece suit at an hour of the morning when most people are still twisted up in their bedsheets, glanced in Gertie's direction before moving forward a bit to see who wanted him. "Well, hello, Mrs. Nash. I didn't know you were watching Lawrence's dog." Lawrence was Gertie's older brother. "He must've got called away on business again."

"That's right." Gertie strained her neck in an effort to speak to the young man further—he stood six feet tall. "They gave him an hour's notice this time. From what I've seen of his yard this morning, it looks like Rascal's not the only one needing care. His lawn could also use some tending to by my Ralphie. Say, Jasper, dear, I hope you don't mind my asking, but what's wrong with your Uncle Charlie? He doesn't seem to be himself today."

The well-groomed man with thick, straight, black hair seemed hesitant to reply. "Jute and I don't like to talk about his problem, especially around him, but these childlike episodes of his seem to be occurring more frequently."

"Really? What kind of episodes, if you don't mind my asking?" Gertie inquired, thinking not only of Charlie's safety but also that of the people on his block. "Nothing dangerous, I hope."

Jasper let loose with a girlish laugh. "Heavens, no. It's not dementia. His problem stems from being struck on the head years ago by sheets of metal when he was in the process of creating a phenomenal sculpture for the Anoka courthouse. Charlie didn't say anything to upset you, did he, Gertie?"

A thorny branch irritated the woman's arm. She pulled it back before it drew blood. "No, but he did say something quite strange."

"What's that?"

"He said someone poisoned someone."

Jasper flicked his hand. "Not that again. I'm afraid he's referring to his black lab from childhood. The farm he grew up on had an abundance of gophers. The only way grandpa knew to rid himself of those varmints was to stuff poison pellets down the holes. Unfortunately, the dog dug them up and ate them."

Gertie got teary-eyed. "How sad. Being a pet owner myself, I can understand how the loss could deeply affect someone. Well, I'd better get Rascal in so he can have his doggy treats. Give your brother Jute my regards. See you later." She scooped Rascal off the ground and walked toward her brother's house.

Just as she snapped back the wooden screen door, Jasper shouted a delicious message across the hedges. "By the way, Gertie, you and Ralph are invited to our next soiree in two weeks. It's always a big hit with the neighbors."

"I'm sure it is, with all the food you two chefs concoct. Thanks for the invite. I'll be sure to come. Speaking of food, tell Jute to stop by tonight. I have a divine recipe you're going to want to offer your restaurant customers. It's to die for."

"Ooooh, right up our alley. I can't wait to try it."

The second Gertie opened the back door to Lawrence's house, her cell phone rang. It was sitting where she had left it when she arrived earlier this morning, on the kitchen counter closest to the back entrance. She set

Rascal down as fast as she could without causing him to slip on the newly tiled kitchen floor and then collected her phone. "Why, hello, Lawrence. I'm surprised to hear from you this early. What's that? You're taking a coffee break. Well, lucky you. I haven't even had my first cup yet."

Lawrence's cheery voice echoed through the phone lines. "Is Rascal being a pest?"

"No, no. He's fine. My morning routine got delayed because I was speaking with Jasper, your next door neighbor. It's so sad about his Uncle Charlie. Did you know he's slowly losing his mind?"

"Oh, the poor man. I didn't know. The few times I've spoken to him he seemed lucid enough. Look, I need to ask a favor. The corporate office wants me to spend two extra days here to receive training on new products soon to be released. Do you think Ralph will mind your being gone longer?"

Gertie splayed her fingers across her neck. "Not at all. He can come here for his suppers; we don't live that far away. By the way, I'm going to ask him to mow your lawn so you don't have to worry about it."

"Thanks. Ralph shouldn't have trouble using the lawn mower. It's been running fine."

"Well, if he does, he can bring ours over. Oh, guess what? Ralph and I've been invited to the annual dinner party the twins put on. I'm going to bring a specialty dish, of course."

"That'll be fun. I can hardly wait to show you the inside of their house. Don't forget, when I get back to Minnesota I'm treating you two to an evening out at a fancy restaurant."

The mere thought of delicious restaurant food made Gertie giddy. She and Ralph rarely ate out. "You're such a dear. See you soon. Enjoy California."

Around nine that evening, Jute, Jasper's identical twin, stopped by to see Gertie. He had changed out of his usual chef's whites into a tan tank top and matching khaki shorts, the type you'd find at any Old Navy store. His long, black, damp hair was pulled back with a binder, exposing one small gold earring looped in his ear. A matching one pierced his narrow nostrils.

Noticing how sweaty her tall visitor appeared when she greeted him at the back door, Gertie graciously offered to retrieve a cold bottle of beer from Lawrence's stash in the fridge while Rascal kept him occupied with his ball. "Such a pest, that dog, but he's good company," Gertie admitted, carrying Jute's opened bottle of beer to the kitchen table where he sat waiting.

"Here you go. This should cool you down nicely."

"Thanks, Gertie. I've always wanted to try Nordeast, but Jasper's such a wine snob." Jute pressed the bottle against his temple for a second. "I can't believe it's been in the 90's for over two weeks. You'd think we lived in Florida, not Minnesota." He brought the bottle down to his soft, rolling lips, took a sip, and then set the bottle down in front of him. "Hmm, nice. So, what's this I hear about a super recipe you're willing to divulge?"

Gertie tapped her painted nails together. "Ah, yes, I acquired it recently from one of Ralph's relatives out east. I planned to give you a copy tonight, but I've changed my mind. I'm going to hold off till your party in two weeks. I'm bringing it for everyone to taste. Then you can see for yourself how everyone loves it."

Jute took another sip of his beer. "Oh, you're the naughty temptress, aren't you, Gertie? Getting me over here on a sweltering night with promises to share a new delight, and then denying me that pleasure. Your recipe better be worth the wait."

Gertie batted her heavily coated lashes. "Oh, believe me, it is."

The night Charlie's nephews were hosting the dinner bash, Jasper floated to the door decked out in the same two-piece suit Gertie had seen him in two weeks earlier. Jute, who trailed a few feet behind him offering before-dinner cocktails, was suited exactly the same down to the dress socks, shoes, and belt.

"Come on in, everyone!" Jasper said, presumably hyped up on sampling too much wine before his guests started arriving. "Glad you could make it."

"Lawrence, Ralph, and Gertie, grab a Banana Caipirnha," Jute said, "There's plenty more in the kitchen."

The three of them obeyed. Each took an elegant brandy glass filled with a minty-flavored banana drink off the tray Jute held out to them, and then moved into the living room, making way for the guests arriving right behind them.

Charlie Sassafrass, dressed in a simple pair of white trousers and a Hawaiian shirt, appeared to be the only one in the room. He sat in a heavy leather recliner near the fireplace adorned with heads of big game trophies. A plate filled with interesting appetizers rested in his lap. "Make sure to get some hors d'oeuvres before they disappear," he said with a smirk when he saw the others.

"We will," Gertie's brother replied, "but I was wondering if I could show my sister and her husband around first before the house fills with guests."

"Certainly. I don't mind. Start with the kitchen," he said with an acidic ring to his voice. "It's where Jasper and Jute spent the majority of my money."

"That's a fabulous idea," Gertie said, still holding the bag containing her surprise dessert. "I can't free up my hands for appetizers if I'm traipsing all over the house with this. It should be in the kitchen with the main course."

Thirty minutes after the last guest arrived, the two chefs, now clothed in their cooking uniforms, rounded up their sixteen guests and asked them to take their seats in the dining room, where they'd find two long rectangular tables covered with white cloths.

Gertie, who had never attended the annual party before, was quite impressed with the elegant china settings, sterling silver, and low floral arrangements decorating each table. "My goodness, I feel like I'm dining with royalty tonight," she whispered in her husband's ear.

Ralph laughed. "I always liked stories about King Arthur. Perhaps I'm from a long line of knights."

"In your dreams," Gertie said under her breath, "Come on, Ralph, help me find our place cards."

"If you came with a significant other tonight," Jasper said in a cheery tone, "you'll notice we mixed up the seating arrangements so you don't have to bore one another. Now make yourselves comfortable while Jute and I get the first course ready."

Gertie found her seat and immediately began chatting with the man to the right of her, who appeared to be around her age. "I see my brother Lawrence and my husband ended up at the other table. How about you, anyone from your household end up there?"

"Nope. I've been divorced for ten years."

"Oh? Sorry I asked."

"Don't be," the man replied. "We got married too young, that's all."

"I bet you enjoy these annual dinner gatherings as much as Lawrence does, then. Did you have a chance to try the stuffed grape leaves and the smoked salmon mousse? I went back for seconds, I couldn't help myself."

The man with the white hair, side burns, neatly trimmed goatee, and mustache gave Gertie a pleasant smile. "I'm afraid I got too busy chatting with my neighbors. By the time I got around to taste anything, the only appetizer left was the asparagus wrapped in crisp prosciutto."

"What did you think?" she inquired.

"Well, I'm no chef or food critic, but I'd have to say I wouldn't mind having it again."

Gertie glanced at the man's name card. "So, what do you do for a living, Mr. Beau Hunter?"

Beau pinched his goatee. "Promise you won't laugh?"

Gertie raised her hand. "I swear."

"I'm a bounty hunter by day and collect antique washing machines on the side."

"My, my, sounds like an interesting life. My husband Ralph and I no longer work, but we do keep ourselves busy visiting wineries. I suppose you've heard Lawrence hunts for edible mushrooms." Beau nodded. "As a matter of fact," Gertie said, folding her arms, "I believe the soup being served tonight contains mushrooms he specifically collected for this occasion."

"Really? So, tell me, Gertie, what influenced your decision to get those cool tattoos on your arms and neck? You must be a huge *Star Wars* fan."

"You'd better believe it. I know you can't see everything, but from the neck down I'm covered with the likes of R2-D2, Darth Vader, C-3PO, and Princess Leia."

"George Lucas sure made some spectacular movies."

"He sure did."

The first course finally came: poached pears soaking in a red wine sauce served in goblets that matched the china. Any further conversation dealing with movies and great film directors was temporarily cut off.

After Jute made sure everyone was taken care of, he stood at the far corner of Gertie's table, watching his guests eat his creation. "Slow down. Don't rush the experience," Jute warned. "Let the wine and pear mingle in your mouth for a while."

"Hmm, I really like this, Jute," Gertie said. "Is this your recipe?"

"Yes. The next one's Jasper's." Jute waited until everyone's pear had been devoured, then he rushed back to join his twin in the kitchen.

Beau turned to Gertie. "I suppose the mushroom soup's next."

"I assume so, unless those two have something else up their sleeves."

Jasper and Jute soon came into view, rolling a cart toward the dining room and their dinner guests. A huge glass soup tureen and soup ladle sat on the top shelf. When they reached the first table, the chefs stopped and began filling each person's soup bowl. "Thanks to Lawrence, tonight's soup is Wild Rice Mushroom," Jasper announced.

"Sounds delicious," Ralph Nash piped up from his table. "I can hardly wait to taste it."

A male dinner guest sitting across from Ralph said, "Don't bother giving me any, Jasper. I'm allergic to dairy products."

"That's fine," Jasper said, not displaying any emotion one way or the other from the news just shared. "I'll see what else I can whip up for you."

"Thanks."

When Jasper returned to the kitchen, scrambling to find something to serve his dinner guest with dairy allergies, he spied Gertie's dessert, which he had set aside for himself and his brother earlier, and decided to sneak a taste. The moment he slid the pineapple dessert into his mouth, he knew he'd be serving this to their customers. "Here, Jute, try what Gertie brought, it's delicious."

"Not right now. I've got to get the salad dressing mixed."

"Oh, that can wait one minute. Just take a bite. It's to die for, like Gertie said." Gertie stacked Beau's and her soup bowls together before grabbing a few more oyster crackers.

"I wonder what's taking them so long in the kitchen," she said. "Jasper was supposed to bring something else for the gentleman sitting by my husband, and the poor man's still waiting."

Beau glanced at his watch. "Maybe they ran out of bowls to put the salads in."

"Hmm? Maybe this lull in courses is a good time to use the powder room," Gertie said, pushing her chair away from the table.

"Why don't you take a peek in the kitchen while you're at it," Beau suggested, "Maybe if they see you they'll hurry the next course along."

"That's a splendid idea."

Gertie entered the half bath from the hallway, but after she finished freshening up her makeup she choose to leave by the door leading to the kitchen. When she stepped into the room, she didn't see the twins slaving away, just Caesar salads waiting to be served on the huge granite counter. Hungry, she strolled over to the prepared salads, snatched some greens from one of the bowls, and munched on them before she made her boldest move, stealing a peek at the main entrée simmering on the six burner gas range on the other side of the counter.

As Gertie finished her last bite of greens, Charlie Sassafrass strolled into the kitchen, cutting short any chance she might have had to take a look at what sat in the huge pots on the stove. "What's going on in here? Where are Jasper and Jute?"

"I don't know," Gertie replied, feeling guilty about eating the greens, "but I think I should turn the burners off before the food is scorched, don't you?"

"Go ahead."

Gertie waddled around the corner and let out a thunderous scream.

"I'm telling you, Officer, I didn't see or hear anything before I entered the kitchen," Gertie said, trying to remain calm while repeating her story yet again a week after Jasper and Jute's death. "Charlie, their uncle, was in the kitchen with me when I discovered their bodies. He'll tell you how upset I was."

Officer Murphy rubbed his wide chin "You're not denying you brought the baked pineapple dish, are you?"

"Why would I? It's a great dish. Who wouldn't enjoy eating a surprising dessert filled with pineapple, grated cheddar, and crushed Hi Ho's? I just can't believe Jasper and Jute tried it before the rest of us. Have you figured out cause of death yet?"

"We believe they were poisoned."

Gertie's chunky hands flew to her cheeks. "Oh, my!"

On the way home from the police station, Gertie stopped by Charlie's to see how he was coping with the twins' death. "Come in and sit a spell," he said. "I'll make you a cup of tea."

"Charlie, is there anything Lawrence or I can do for you now that the twins are gone?"

The elderly man plopped a cup of tea in front of Gertie. "Heck, no. It's a relief to have them gone."

Shocked to hear Charlie Sassafrass speak so coldly of his nephews, whom Gertie thought he loved, she questioned what he meant.

"Jasper and Jute were scheming all the time. They sat in my kitchen night after night discussing which restaurant they'd destroy next, while going deeper into debt. Some was just talk, but I wonder. Anyway, when I got wind of their scheme to do away with me using the new street drug Flakka so they could inherit my house and all my money, I said to myself, 'Charlie, Enough is enough. I'll show those two spoiled brats.' And

I did, didn't I? They never saw it coming. After they busied themselves with the second course in the dining room, I snuck into the kitchen and put gopher poison in both their sample bowls. If I've learned one thing living with chefs, it's that they like to taste everything before it's served to others."

CHICKEN WILD RICE SOUP

Courtesy of Keys Café and Bakery, Roseville location (www.keyscafe.com)

DIRECTIONS

- Celery, onions, carrots chopped and cooked in chicken or turkey base.
- Add cooked wild rice.
- Salt, pepper, chicken base, sweet basil, and cayenne.
- Add heavy cream and chicken or turkey.
- Thicken with roux.

The Way to a Man's Heart

BY WENDY WEBB

A STIFF OCTOBER wind swirled through the streets of downtown Minneapolis as Matthew Wright sat behind his desk at Antiquarian Books and Other Oddities, a quirky shop tucked into a corner of a dusty, old, renovated warehouse in the trendy North Loop neighborhood. He was engrossed in paperwork from his recent trip to Romania to buy a first edition of *Dracula* for a client—it's what he specialized in, traveling the world to find rare, valuable, and precious volumes for wealthy collectors—when a shock of cold air rushed into the shop and told him that he was no longer alone.

He looked up to find a woman standing in front of his desk, a grey shawl pulled around her.

Matthew smiled. "Feel free to browse," he said. "You'll find a lot of interesting treasures here. Rare books. Antiques."

But she just stood there, blinking, looking from his face to the floor and back again. Finally, she coughed into her hand and said: "Actually, I'm looking for something specific." Her gaze fell to the floor and stayed there.

The air in the shop seemed to thicken then, and a tendril of chill ran up Matthew's spine. He was no stranger to being approached by wary clients, but when one of them wouldn't even meet his gaze . . . it never signaled anything good. Either they wouldn't have the funds to pay, were up to something illegal—running some kind of scam—or, most likely, they were looking for information that would allow them to delve into realms he would prefer to stay out of. Dark realms. Voodoo. Magic. Worse than that. He had learned all too well over the years that ancient books contained secrets. Forgotten knowledge that people would pay handsomely to acquire.

This woman was no scammer—he could spot them a mile away. She was seeking something dark and dangerous, he could smell it on her. And see it in her manner. Stooped posture. Downcast eyes. The way she was biting her lip. He had seen that look before, with disastrous results. If he took on this client, he'd be going down the rabbit hole. Again.

He cleared his throat. "What can I help you with, exactly?"

"This might sound a little strange to you," she began, gingerly meeting his gaze.

"Believe me, honey, I've heard it all," Matthew said, glancing down at his watch. "Now, why don't you just tell me what it is, and I'll tell you whether I can help you or not."

"I want a book of spells." Her eyes were shining now.

"Magic spells?"

She narrowed those shining eyes at him. "Is there any other kind?" She shuffled closer to the desk and lowered her voice, as if to take him into her confidence. "I want a powerful love spell. Genuine. Guaranteed to work. I want to compel a man, a certain man, to love me."

Matthew shook his head. Usually his clients didn't blurt out their reasons for wanting any particular volume. He had adopted a policy of complete discretion over many years and many clients. The wealthy appreciated it, and frankly he thought their reasons were none of his business, unless they were going to do something illegal or, God forbid, burn or destroy the book. In those cases, he wouldn't help them.

"Your charm and beauty aren't enough? Surely . . ."

"No!" the woman broke in. "I love him and . . ." Her words trailed off.

"He doesn't share your feelings."

"I'm so tired of always being shuttled into the friend zone," she went on. "I don't want to be this man's friend. I want to be his everything. I know that, deep down, he wants it, too."

Oh, honey, honey, honey, Matthew thought. *That's the oldest lie in the world.*

Matthew let out a long sigh and ran a hand through his hair. "I don't recommend—"

"I didn't come here for your recommendation," she hissed. "I came here for a spell book."

"I don't have anything like that in stock," he huffed, waiting a moment before continuing. "But I do know where I might get it. How much are you willing to pay?"

"What do you charge?"

"Not only for the book, for starters. For my time, travel, and labor. It's not easy to acquire these ancient texts. Cajoling is involved. Wining and dining. Charming. Convincing. Collectors don't like to give up their treasures. Money is not the only thing."

"Again, I'm asking you, what do you charge?" This time she held his gaze.

Matthew did some quick mental calculations. The woman he was intending to see was in Massachusetts. It would mean a flight to Boston, a rental car, a hotel. Hours of talking. Last time he was at this woman's house, there were upwards of twenty cats roaming around. He tacked on some hazard pay for that. And then the spell book itself, an ancient volume having its roots in the darkest of the Commonwealth's history. He had no idea what she would charge him for that.

"We might be talking about six figures, depending on what this collector will charge me for the book, if I can even get it," he said, hoping in the back of his mind this would be the end of it.

She nodded. "I can do that."

Groan. "Okay," he said. "I'll tell you what. You think about this thing overnight. I don't care if you came for a recommendation or not, you're getting one. This is not a good idea. I cannot possibly guarantee the authenticity of the spells in this book. I don't believe in magic, for one thing, but for another, my business is acquiring and selling ancient, rare books and other treasures. I can guarantee that this—if I'm even able to get it—will be an ancient book. That's all. You cannot come back to me asking for a refund when you don't get the results you want. Do you understand that?"

"I understand."

"I'll need $10,000 upfront and the rest when I deliver the book."

She pulled her shawl around her and turned to go. "I'll see you to-morrow."

"I want you to go into this with your eyes open," he called after her.

But his words evaporated in the cold air as she walked out the door.

Anna hurried down the busy street away from Matthew's shop, thrilled that he had bought her sob story about unrequited love. To be fair, it was partially true. The man she loved had spurned her for another woman. And it was true that she wanted to make him love her again. But not to live the rest of her life with him. No, she wanted revenge. She was burning with it. She wanted to make him feel the way she felt when she found him with her months ago. It was, really, a sin of omission, her not telling Matthew the whole truth. Not a lie, exactly. What was it his business anyway? He was just the middle man. She smiled as she pulled her shawl tighter around her and hurried home, her pace lightening with every step.

Two days later, Matthew was driving from the Boston airport to Con-cord, a town steeped in both Revolutionary War history as well as Amer-ican literary history. The Battle of Lexington and Concord was the first of the Revolutionary War. The town was also home to Ralph Waldo Em-erson, Henry David Thoreau (Walden Pond sat nearby), and Nathanial Hawthorne. Louisa May Alcott wrote Little Women in her family home in Concord, now a museum. Literary genius seemed to waft through the air there. It was a bright, blue day, and the fall colors were intense and blazing. There was nothing like fall in New England, Matthew thought as he drove.

Not far outside of the town center, Matthew pulled up outside a massive wooden house with a typical New England-style stone fence running the length of the property, acres and acres of it. Enormous, ancient trees hadn't yet shed their bright leaves. Geese drifted along on a pond adjacent to the house. Cats prowled in the field beyond. Pumpkins lined the driveway. It was a perfect autumn day in Concord, but as Matthew turned into the drive, his stomach did a quick flip. He wasn't afraid, not exactly, but the woman he was meeting always gave him a little pause.

He was never quite sure if she was friend or foe.

Elizabeth Stone was the High Priestess of a large coven with ancient roots dating back to the darkest times in Massachusetts history. To hear her tell it, the intense patriotism and fortitude the colonists needed to fight the British came from a spell the coven cast on the town. Likewise, the lure that drew and inspired the most accomplished writers of the day.

She was standing on her front porch as Matthew pulled up to the house. Her appearance always surprised him a bit. He imagined that she'd be in a long dress or a robe, given who she was, but today she was leaning against the wrought iron railing wearing a fisherman's knit sweater and jeans. She waved at him and smiled.

"Welcome, my friend," she said as he scrambled out of the car.

"Thank you for seeing me on such short notice," he said, trotting up the stone steps and enveloping her in a hug.

"I know you just wanted an excuse to come to Concord in the fall," she said with a grin.

"Any excuse to see you is a fine one," he said, smiling his best smile.

She threaded her arm through his and ushered him inside. On previous visits, they always conducted their business in the drawing room, but on this day she steered him toward the kitchen. Cats scurried through the hallways as they walked to the back of the house, where she pushed open a door to what was obviously the heart of their home.

A long, wooden table sat in front of a wall of windows looking out onto the pond near the house. A massive stove stood on the opposite wall, copper pots and pans hanging above it.

Cookbooks lined a bookshelf, a teapot was boiling on the stove, and jackets were draped on hooks next to the back door, boots beside it.

"Please do sit down," she said, gesturing toward the table. "Tea?"

"I'd love some," he said, peeling off his jacket.

Elizabeth poured steaming water into two mugs and handed one to Matthew as she sank into a chair beside him. "It's my own blend," she said. "I think you'll like it."

"I'll just let it cool a bit," he said, eyeing the mug. Her own blend, indeed.

After a few minutes of small talk, she turned to him, her face suddenly serious and stern.

"I do have what you're seeking," she said.

Matthew held his breath. He knew better than to talk too much during this phase of the transaction. He was going to let her do what she was going to do, say what she was going to say.

She pushed back her chair and crossed the room to the bookshelf. She ran her finger along the spines of books and pulled one out. "Here it is," she said, setting the book on the table in front of him.

Matthew knew this book dated back a century if not more, but its leather cover was in good shape—eerily good shape. He leafed through a few pages and then looked up at Elizabeth, wrinkling his nose.

"I'm confused," he said. "I asked you for a spell book. This is a cookbook."

Elizabeth smiled. "Yes. It is. They are one and the same."

"I don't get it."

"In the old days, women would come to my ancestors for a variety of reasons, but many of them had to do with their husbands, or the men who they wanted," she said, sinking back down into her chair and stroking the cover of the book. "Their husbands beat them and they wanted it to stop. Their husbands were cold and unloving, and they wanted to feel the warmth of a man's arms around them. The man they adored wanted someone else. They were unable to bear children. They came to us for help when they were desperate. We were always their last resort."

As she was talking, he was sipping his tea. And all at once, he blinked a long, heavy blink. Matthew wanted nothing but to close his eyes. He did, just for a moment, and an image floated into his mind. He saw Elizabeth wearing a long dress, her hair pulled back into a bun. She was standing at the stove, stirring a pot and writing down the recipe as she added ingredients. Then he saw a woman in a dark cloak knocking on the back door of this kitchen, looking this way and that to make sure nobody had followed her. Elizabeth opened the door and ushered the woman inside. The two sat at the table where Matthew was sitting and talked, the woman crying, Elizabeth nodding. Finally, she opened the book and flipped through the pages until she found the recipe she wanted. She lifted the page out of the book and as she did so, another materialized in its place. She handed the loose page to the woman.

Then the image faded, and Matthew was back in the kitchen again. He opened his eyes and squinted at Elizabeth.

"So, you have seen," she said.

"What did you . . ." Matthew started, and then scowled at his teacup.

Elizabeth smiled. "I thought a visual would be easier than a long explanation," she said. "You know what happened to witches back in the day, especially here. It was vital we weren't discovered, so instead of traditional spells, we created recipes with very specific combinations of ingredients to achieve what the women wanted to achieve."

She opened the book and paged through it. "Your client wants to make a man love her, is that right? They are not married."

"That's right."

"Why does she want to do this thing?" Elizabeth asked, her eyes dark. "Why compel someone to love you, who doesn't?"

Matthew shrugged. "She says she's in the friend zone and wants to be his everything."

"She wants to be his everything," Elizabeth whispered, closing her eyes. "His everything. Yes, I think I can make that happen."

She lifted a recipe out of the book and Matthew watched as an identical page materialized in its place. He scowled down at his tea again. What had she put in it?

She handed the page to Matthew.

"Wait, so I'm not getting the book?" he asked. "Just this recipe?"

Elizabeth nodded. "I would never let the book leave this house," she said. "It has been serving women in this area for generations. Centuries. My ancestors added to it when they developed new recipes, as did my grandmother and mother before me. As do I. It stays here."

"But . . ." Matthew started. But he knew it was no use. She wouldn't give up the book for any price. He eyed the recipe. Harvest Stew. Meat simmered in beer and beef broth. It sounded delicious.

"The recipe is all she needs," Elizabeth said. "A combination of the right ingredients and her focused intention will manifest what she desires.

"*He doesn't have any idea what she most desires,*" Elizabeth said silently to one of her cats.

She pushed her chair away from the table and crossed the room to a large, built-in buffet with dozens of small drawers, much like one Matthew had seen in an apothecary shop in Hungary the year before. He watched as Elizabeth opened one of the drawers and pulled out a small cheesecloth bag. She began whispering words Matthew didn't understand as she opened another, plucked out some dried herbs and dropped them in the bag, and repeated the process a few more times, opening other drawers and pulling out other herbs. She placed a dried sprig of something—thyme?—onto a smooth, flat stone and lit the sprig on fire, capturing the pungent-smelling smoke into the bag. She let it burn to ashes, scooped them up, and put them in the bag as well. Next came a vial. One, two, three drops fell into the bag.

Elizabeth tied it shut, turned, and handed the bag to Matthew.

"Tell her to use this to season the stew, and to think about what she wants—what she truly wants—over and over again like a mantra, as she's cooking it," she said. "If she doesn't, it'll just be a delicious meal. With this, it's a powerful potion. Anyone who eats it will fall in love with the person who cooked it. So tell her it's best she doesn't throw a dinner party." A slight smile crept onto her face.

Matthew nodded. "So that's it? The herbs and the recipe."

"Yes," she said. "But there's one more thing she should know. Dabbling in magic can be very dangerous. It is an unpredictable force for people who aren't skilled artisans. Tell her to be very careful and very precise in terms of what she wishes for. It could have disastrous results."

Matthew's stomach turned again. "Got it," he said.

They agreed on a modest price—he would certainly give some of his advance back to Anna—which he paid in cash. Then she took his hands in hers and said: "And now this deal is done."

A shock of electricity ran through Matthew's body as she said it. It made him wonder who, exactly, he had made this deal with.

Anna held the cheesecloth bag as she read the recipe. It sounded delicious—cubed beef, caramelized onions, and root vegetables simmered in beef broth and beer, topped with bubbling Swiss cheese, and served with crusty French bread. French onion soup on steroids.

He was coming to her house at six o'clock for dinner. It had taken some cajoling, but he finally agreed when she told him she wanted to talk about a mutual friend who was in trouble. It was a white lie, but she had to get him there somehow. No matter. It would all be forgotten when he was aching for her and she was rejecting him. Ooo, maybe he'd leave his current girlfriend for her. Wouldn't that be delicious?

She thought about it as she sliced the onions and cubed the beef, rutabaga and butternut squash. As the veggies were roasting in the oven, she sautéed the onions, thinking about him. Maybe she'd string him along awhile. She added the beef, the beer, and the broth and dropped the cheesecloth bag into the stew, imagining his sad face when she told him it was over.

She couldn't wait for six o'clock to arrive.

• • • • •

A few weeks later, Anna burst through the door of Matthew's shop and rushed up to his desk, out of breath.

"You've got to help me," she said, her voice torn to shreds. "I've got to reverse this thing."

"Reverse it? So it actually worked? You're kidding me."

Anna slapped one hand on his desk. "Hell yes, it worked. Too well! He's at my place all the time. He won't leave!"

Matthew scowled, not quite believing her. "But that's what you wanted, right? Are you sure you're not overreacting?"

"You don't get it. He's following me everywhere, coming to my workplace and just standing outside my window like a stalker." She swallowed, hard. "My best friend went missing a couple of days ago. Nobody's heard from her. When I asked him about it, he just laughed. And that's not all. It's like there's something . . ."

Matthew leaned in. "What?"

Anna leaned in, too, and Matthew could feel the panic that surrounded her.

"His eyes changed color," she whispered. "Right after eating the stew. I swear to God I watched them change from blue to black. It's almost like there's something inside of him now. Something that wasn't there before."

A shiver ran up Matthew's spine. He thought about Elizabeth's warning.

"This is my fault," she said. "I wanted revenge. I wanted to make him love me so I could dump him the way he dumped me."

Matthew groaned. "Don't even . . ."

"He's dangerous," she went on. "And he's coming after me."

"Anna, are you afraid of this man?"

"I don't think it's a man anymore," she whispered.

And that's when Matthew saw him, standing out on the sidewalk, staring at them through the window, his inky eyes shining, a slight smile on his face. He was carrying a walking stick. All at once Matthew knew Anna was right. Her dark motives and Elizabeth's dark magic had intertwined to create something horrible. This man wasn't alive anymore.

There was no soul behind those eyes.

Matthew picked up the phone to dial 911 just as the window shattered.

ELIZABETH'S HARVEST STEW

INGREDIENTS

- 3 strips of bacon
- Unsalted butter
- Olive oil
- 2-3 lbs. steak
- 2 tbsp. of flour
- 3 yellow onions
- 1 cup carrots, cubed
- ½-1 cup rutabaga, cubed
- 1 cup butternut squash, cubed
- Thyme
- 1 bottle Guinness or other dark beer
- 32 oz. beef broth
- Sliced Swiss cheese
- French bread

DIRECTIONS

Preheat the oven to 425 degrees. Cook the bacon in a Dutch oven or large stew pot. When the bacon is done, remove it and enjoy this treat for the cook. Add 3-4 tbsp. of butter to the pot. When it's melted, add the sliced onions and sauté over medium to low heat until they caramelize. (Plan on about 30 minutes, and stir them every now and then.) Cube the other veggies and pop them into a resalable plastic bag. Drizzle them with olive oil, seal the bag, and shake it up. Spill the veggies out of the bag and onto a cookie sheet lined with foil. Roast the veggies in the oven for about 20 minutes. They're done when they brown a little bit and are soft but not mushy. When done, remove from the oven and set aside. While the onions are doing their thing and the veggies are roasting, cube the meat into bite-size pieces.

When the onions are done, remove them from the pot and set aside. Put the meat into the pot and brown it a bit, then add the flour and cook for a minute or two. Then add the beer, deglazing the bottom of the pot as you go. (That's just scraping up anything sticking to the bottom.) Add the onions back in and add enough broth to cover it all. Add the thyme and pepper to taste. Cover and simmer for 90 minutes. Add the roasted veggies and simmer for another 30 minutes.

Slice the French bread so you have 1 to 2 slices per bowl. Place slices on the cookie sheet, put a slice or two of Swiss cheese on each one, and broil until the cheese is bubbly. Ladle the stew into bowls, top each one with the cheesy French bread, and ladle a little sauce on top of that.

The Debut of Reggie Smalls

BY MICHAEL SEARS

ANGIE AND THE KID had colds and our Tribeca apartment smelled like menthol. I don't know why I wasn't sick, too. I wasn't sleeping, and the daily stress of covering up a ballooning accounting fraud was chipping away at my immune system. I felt like a zombie with a caffeine buzz.

"I'm spending the weekend in Montauk. Maybe that'll keep me from catching whatever it is you two have got."

Angie's eyes were red and watery. Was it vodka or the virus? "Whatever," she croaked.

Maybe she knew I was lying. I might sleep in Montauk, but there was a party in East Hampton I planned on attending first.

The invitation came from Zeki Toraman, the man who had founded Ad Astra, currently the world's fourth largest hedge fund. Every fall, Mr. Toraman threw an end-of-year extravaganza at his beach house for members of the industry. As a mere trading manager at a bank, I was too far down the totem pole to ever have been invited before. There was no obvious reason for me to have been invited this year. That meant that someone had made a very deliberate choice to include me. I was intrigued.

The line of limos waiting to get through the gates was backed up to Further Lane. My Town Car stuck out for being the smallest vehicle in sight. The mammoth in front of us was a U.S. Army personnel carrier, stretched out an extra few feet and painted in matte graphite gray. It looked like a stealth bomber mounted on five-foot wheels. The out of state license plate read LEVERAGE.

A white-gloved, tuxedoed man with the build of a SmackDown! Superstar held the door for me, checked my name—and face—on a laptop, and directed me to a seat on an electric wagon that carried eight of us up the driveway to the house.

The grounds were lit with pots and spots, highlighting an assortment of non-native vegetation. My house in Montauk was surrounded by cattails, scrub oak, and pine, and I liked it that way. The plants weren't pretty or exotic, but I didn't have to pay a gardener more than twice a year to cut back the poison ivy. I shook my head. Why own a beachfront home if you wanted it to look like high-end California suburbia? There was a pool with a cabana the size of a two-bedroom house; a series of putting greens surrounded by sand traps and a man-made stream that circulated over a miniature waterfall; a stable and riding ring; and, of course, clay tennis courts and a croquet court.

The house was just as confusing. It was huge, of course, but the surprise was that it was boring. Plain as a tract home in Lake Grove. The portico was designed to be impressive, with two-story columns over eight-foot double doors, but it had the feel of having been tacked on as an afterthought. The lines were boxy. There were plenty of windows, but they were set in military precision, with no variation. The place was custom-built for someone with no architectural taste, no eye for beauty. But it was huge.

The doors opened and we filed up the long stone steps in ones and twos. I stepped through the portal into a main hall whose ceiling arched up three stories. A third of a football field away, a glass wall gave out onto a Versailles-sized veranda and, presumably, the Atlantic Ocean. On either side, staircases swept up to the upper floors. The room was meant to impress, and it succeeded admirably.

Mr. Toraman was flanked by a pair of tuxedoed staff, both armed with laptops of their own. As I approached, I read one's lips as he announced me in a confidential whisper to his boss.

"Jason Stafford."

"Jason," Zeki roared in exaggerated pleasure. "I am so glad you could come. There are people here you should meet. Have a glass of bourbon and join the crowd. We'll talk later."

Another liveried man handed me a tumbler with a single golf-ball sized ice cube and began pouring from a bottle of Pappy Van Winkle. "Say when," he said.

"When!" I said. It was a very generous pour and I was not a whiskey drinker.

Zeki was already engaged with the two men behind me, so I moved on into the hallway.

A haze of cigar smoke hung over the noisy crowd—all men. There were no women in evidence, among either the guests or the staff.

"Stafford, isn't it? You're the currency guy at Case."

The speaker was a hawk-faced young man with a black widow's peak. I put his age at a few years my junior. His youth made me realize that he and I were among the youngest at the party. The average attendee was already showing some gray hairs and facial stress lines.

"Jason Stafford," I said. I put out a hand to shake.

He ignored it. "We don't see many bank people at these gatherings." He made the word bank sound like a slur.

"We've never met, have we?" I asked. Rudeness from traders is rarely personal, so I chose to ignore it.

"You gave a class on foreign exchange when I was in the training program."

I gave one lecture a year to the new hires. Some were destined for sales or trading, but the vast majority were headed for traditional banking, from branch management to corporate lending to investment banking. The lecture was a one-size-fits-all garment, which, no doubt, satisfied no one.

"You're no longer with the firm?" I guessed by his attitude.

"Too much bureaucracy. Too many lawyers. Too many executives looking over your shoulder."

"Yeah, well, we train the best and keep the rest."

"So what are you doing here? This is a party for hedge fund managers and top executives. You're not thinking of going to the dark side, are you?"

"I didn't get your name." I was fed up with the attitude. There must have been someone—anyone—I could be talking to other than this clown.

"I'm Reggie Smalls. I thought you knew." Reggie Smalls was the evening's honoree. The highlight of Zeki's yearly parties, as reported in private conversations only, was the feting of the best-performing debut trader in the hedge fund community. Smalls had kicked butt. His fund had started last October with $200 million in investor funds. Hedge funds don't have to divulge all their secrets, but Smalls had claimed in marketing documents that his strategy had something to do with options and inter-market execution—whatever that meant. As of the end of his third quarter in operation, the fund stood at $1.1 billion with no new money. That was a 733% annualized return. No one else had even come close. In fact, it had been a tough year for hedge funds overall. His closest competitor had claimed a banner year at up 54%. More than a few showed negative returns.

"Sorry," I said. "I didn't catch it. Reggie Stahl, did you say?"

He gave me the kind of smile you make when you realize that the glass of milk you just gulped has turned sour and is about to come right back up.

"Smalls. Nice talking to you. Asshole." He turned his back and walked away, rolling his lats like Toshiro Mifune in *Seven Samurai*. If he wasn't such a jerk, it might have been cool.

I felt quite proud of myself for provoking him far enough that he felt that he had to call me names. I looked around for someone else to annoy.

A waiter passed by with a tray of cocktails. I stopped him. "Is it possible to get a light beer? Any light beer."

He shook his head. "Full carb, full alcohol. Craft beers only."

I placed my barely tasted glass of bourbon on his tray. "Bring me a whatever, then."

He nodded and moved on. I surveyed the room again, recognizing three CEOs, a Federal Reserve Governor, and a few other faces that showed up from time to time on Bloomberg News or CNBC. Missing were the superstars like Soros, Steinman, and Paulson.

"Would you care for a lobster roll, sir?" Another waiter was at my elbow with a tray of miniature lobster rolls. Each was about three inches long, but piled with meat and oozing melted butter. I promised myself a long run in the morning and took two.

The hall stretched from front to back of the house. I made my way to the rear glass wall and out into the night. A stone and tile verandah was arranged with two dozen tables, each with eight place settings, the whole area lit like Yankee Stadium. Torches surrounded the eating area. I smelled the combined scents of kerosene, smoking fat from the barbecue grills, citronella candles on each table, and, buried in there somewhere, the unmistakable aroma of salt water. The ocean was steps away, yet I was so blinded by the glare that I had not even noticed.

Once I realized it was there, I focused my senses. I heard the surf before I saw it. The waves were gentle and the sound soothing. My house in Montauk had a water view—if you stood on the roof—but it did not have the surf breaking in the backyard. I could learn to love the sound. Worries sloughed away. I could almost forget the growing disaster I had created at work. Accountants and lawyers were already circling like the vultures they were. They had done nothing to prevent my scam, and little to uncover it, but they would take the credit in the end, picking at my bones, plucking out my eyes, and eating my heart. It was coming. Just a matter of time.

"Your beer, sir." The first waiter had found me. He handed me a bottle of something called Whale Piss. "Would you like a frosted glass?"

I sucked melted butter off of my fingertips. "No, thanks. I'm good," I said.

"I see you're being well-cared for," a voice boomed in my ear. Zeki. And a pinched-face man in a three-button suit wearing tiny rimless glasses. "Can I show you around? Introduce you to some people?"

The only way I was going to find out why I was there was to follow Zeki's lead. "That sounds great, Zeki." I swallowed the last of the second lobster roll and washed it down with a sip of beer. It wasn't a Bud Lite, but it wasn't bad. "I think I'm ready."

"This is Henrik Zondervan. He works for me in research. I want you to help him with a question. Maybe a little later?"

"Pleased to make your acquaintance," the man said. He had a European accent, but I couldn't place the country. I grew up in Queens and have an ear for South and Central American dialects, and can usually tell Chinese from Korean from Thai, but Northern Europe was a blur.

Denmark? Netherlands? Belgium? Not Germany or France. I gave up and shook his hand.

"As long as I'm not giving away Case secrets, I'm happy to help," I said.

"Thank you, Jason. I appreciate the gesture. And now . . . ?" He waved a hand. We went back inside and began working our way through the group.

I wanted to know why I was getting the attention. By all rights, Zeki should have been showing off the rising star, Reggie Smalls. I caught sight of him from time to time as we made our way around the room. He knew he was being snubbed and hated it. There were plenty of others who surrounded him and kept him occupied, but the center of attention in the room was always Zeki and his circle. Smalls shot me hate-laden glances whenever he could catch my eye. The message was easy to read. He wanted to bury me.

Meanwhile, I was being introduced to the upper distillate of Wall Street, and that felt very good. I forgot about Mr. Smalls and why all this was happening. I was surprised at how many of these traders knew my name and were aware of my more legitimate accomplishments. True, I had landed quite a coup a few years back with the Euro conversion, but I was a manager of a small group of FX traders at a bank. These guys controlled trillions. More than a few made more in a day than I earned in a year. I was a millionaire a few times over. Small potatoes in a room with a few dozen billionaires.

Waiters passed with miniature crab cakes, shrimp balls, clam rolls, and more lobster rolls. I had a second beer. I pumped hands with traders I had read about in magazines. I met a professor turned trader whose formulae I had memorized in B-school. He was now worth nearly as much as the endowment of his old school. An engineer, who once designed guidance systems for drones, had created a high-speed trading system and was now telling me about the ocean-front compound he had purchased in Hawaii.

"You must come visit. As soon as my wife is done with the decorating."

Another man laughed. "You said that to me a year ago."

"My wife is very particular," he answered.

All the men laughed.

The professor slipped a business card into my hand and, in an undertone masked by the laughter, said, "Let me buy you lunch someday."

The gesture and words were meant to be private, but all of the men present seemed to recognize what had happened. I was being recruited—by a deity. Zeki nodded his approval, as though this were all a part of his plan for me that evening.

"Dinner will be in half an hour, so drink up, my friends," he called out to the crowd.

"Come with me, Jason. It is time for you to help me."

Finally.

Henrik led the way through a doorway almost hidden behind the swooping staircase and down a short hall. We entered an intimate office the size of my whole uptown apartment. When Henrik closed the door behind us, the air developed the deadened sound of a recording studio—or a vault.

"Good, good. Now we have some privacy and we can talk," Zeki said. He gestured to a leather couch and I sat. Henrik took the other end. Zeki faced me across a coffee table that I first took to be cream-colored plastic. A moment later, I realized with a start that it was made of hundreds of pieces of carved ivory, all fitted together with such perfection that the seams were almost invisible.

"I would like Henrik to take over, if you don't mind. He is the one who first identified this anomaly. He will explain."

Henrik cleared his throat. He dropped the polite European reticence and spoke in a decidedly direct manner. "I am not a trader, you see. But I have been a student of markets since I was a small boy. I have faith in the purity of markets. A faith that is often tried, I admit. So when I see events that do not fit, that stand out in some way, my interest is piqued. You see?"

"And what has piqued your interest?" Traders are less patient than researchers.

"Volatility is our lifeblood. We can only make money when markets are in motion. For the last year, volatility has been historically low. Most of Wall Street—and I include both banks and funds in that description— has had a dreadful time producing the kinds of numbers we need to flourish."

"As J.P. Morgan put it, 'Markets will fluctuate.'"

"Precisely."

Zeki cut in. "Tonight we are to honor a young man who has made the kinds of profits that we rarely see even in very good years. He is new, his fund is relatively small, but to have this kind of luck is beyond any statistical probability. In a word, it is impossible."

Henrik took up the ball. "Maybe not impossible, but certainly improbable. I want to know how he did it."

I laughed. "And why ask me? He trades what? Options on stocks, right? I can tell you a little about options, but nothing you don't already know. I know the difference between delta and gamma, but I don't know squat about the equity market. Not my area. I'm sorry to disappoint."

Wall Street is all about specialization. A trader in one market might be clueless about the job of the guy sitting next to him. Foreign exchange and stocks were worlds apart.

"Well," Henrik continued, "what I did was examine the production of thousands of traders—institutional traders like yourself—to see whether Mr. Smalls was unique or not. He is not. But he is a rarity. And so are you."

A lead refrigerator dropped onto my chest. Blood was pounding so loudly in my ears, I couldn't believe that they didn't hear it. This was it. I was about to be unmasked. Disgraced. I would be lucky just to lose everything I had, if I stayed out of jail. My trading account showed that I was up two hundred million on the year. The reality? Maybe I was up ten. The thing had gotten so far out of control in the last three years that I no longer could keep track of it. It was about to crash and take me with it.

"Would you be willing to just take a few minutes and look at some data that Henrik has discovered? I think you may be the one person who can help." Zeki was polite, polished, and graceful. He wasn't threatening, though I sensed that he would have shown exactly the same cool manner if he were feeding me to the sharks.

I forced myself to speak. "I'd be glad to do whatever I can."

"Good. You are a gentleman."

Henrik crossed to a teak desk that probably outweighed the Town Car I had arrived in, and brought back a laptop. He fired it up, placed it on the ivory table, and spun it so that we could both see the screen.

I found myself looking at a scrolling list of trades. Buys and sells. Open and closing positions. Daily, monthly, and year-to-date profit and loss broken down by security. Exchange-traded options expire four times a year, but you can purchase—or sell—them out into the future. Smalls was very active, trading long, short, and intermediate puts, calls, straddles, and strangles, in every possible combination.

"How the hell did you get this?" I said.

Zeki smiled. Henrik shrugged. He knew, but wasn't going to share.

"Please," he said. "Look carefully. I have examined the data, but it needs a trader's eye. Your eye."

The symbols were meaningless to me. At first. But slowly I began to see patterns. I still didn't have any idea what the guy was trading, but I could apprehend some of his strategies.

Money today is almost always worth more than money deferred. This is called the time value of money, and it is one of the first lessons in finance. This is the basis of the bond market, of futures, options, mortgages, and so on. Reggie Smalls had discovered a way to roll his losses into the future while booking his wins immediately. I could see it quite clearly. I recognized it so easily because it was exactly what I had been doing.

Henrik was talking while I was staring at the screen, explaining the program that he had devised and its results. I missed a lot of the details, but the overall message was that his computer had identified two traders whose results defied credulity, given the state of the markets.

Reggie was one. I was the other.

My options were few. If I pretended not to see the scam, they would think that I was lying—possibly in collusion with Smalls. But if I showed them how the damn thing worked, not only would I be ratting out another trader—though one I found to be thoroughly unpleasant—but I would open myself up to similar accusations. But Henrik was right, and if the accountants at Case had not already found out what I had been doing, they would soon. I made my decision.

"He is making money. Not much, but he's definitely profitable. I'd guess—and it is very much a guess—is that he's up somewhere between eight and ten percent. The rest is bad accounting. And, no, there is no way that it is a simple mistake. It takes a lot of work to keep something like this going. The guy is a con."

Henrik looked troubled. He wanted to be wrong. He wanted to have discovered the hole in his system that revealed the existence of a golden goose, a secret elixir, the fountain of youth, and the goddamn Holy Grail. Zeki just smiled.

"Henrik, would you ask our friends to join us? They need to hear this."

Henrik rose and walked out, his face a solemn mask, as though he were on his way to a wake.

"Can I get you another beer?" Zeki asked.

"I think I'd take a glass of that bourbon, if there's any left."

He got up and opened a cabinet, revealing a full bar. "Ten- or twenty-year-old?"

Both sounded like criminal sentences. "The ten will be fine."

He poured us each a hefty dollop. "Ice?"

"If you're having."

"I take it neat," he said, handing me a glass. "What will you do?"

He knew. He read my face, my body language, probably read my thoughts. "Get a lawyer."

"I can recommend someone."

I nodded. "Thanks."

"If you were to walk away? Take another job? There are people here who would hire you in a New York minute, as they say."

I sighed and shook my head. "I walk, and the whole thing comes apart."

We sipped the bourbon. I doubted that I would grow to love it, but I could taste its appeal.

There was a discrete knock at the door before it swung open. In walked four men whose faces were familiar to anyone who worked on Wall Street. They dropped into the chairs and sofas and all directed their gaze to Zeki.

He met their looks and began. "It is as bad as we imagined. Jason? Would you enlighten us?"

I ran through the trades, showing how Smalls had kept it all rolling. There were a few questions, but mostly they listened. It didn't take long to explain.

The head of the New York Federal Reserve Bank spoke first. "I'll have to get in touch with D.C. He'll want Treasury's okay before we make any commitments."

Zeki nodded, as though this was expected. "The industry cannot afford the scandal right now. We have to finesse this."

The Fed responded, "Oh, I agree. Confidence is at an all-time low. We close him down, settle with his investors, and hope that the goddamn *Times* or the *Guardian* doesn't smell it out."

The chief executive of the world's second largest bank weighed in. "I'll talk to my guy at the *Journal*. He'll spin it our way."

A hedge fund manager who personally owned forty percent of a major cable news station asked, "And what do we do about Smalls?"

"Treasury will insist he gets barred," the Fed answered.

"Can we do that quietly? Just give him five or ten mil and tell him to move to Phu Ket?"

Zeki answered that one. "I am sure that he can be persuaded to take it. The alternative would not be to his liking."

"He's going to walk?" I asked. "No prison time?" I didn't know whether to be hopeful that clemency might extend to me, or repelled that such a fraud would have no repercussions.

The Fed answered. "If this were to happen at a bank, let's say, or a mutual fund, or any publicly owned corporation, we would have to hand this over to Justice and, yes, there would be prison time. But a hedge fund is a private entity. As long as the fund's investors are taken care of, our interests are in keeping this quiet. As Zeki points out, we cannot afford to lose the confidence of the international investment community."

"Suppose he doesn't take it," I said. "Suppose he wants to go public and brazen it out?"

They all shared a look.

Zeki answered for them.

"I would think his health might suffer."

The Fed made a phone call to D.C. while the rest of the group discussed how best to liquidate the fund. Henrik and I kept our mouths shut. They agreed to pay off the fund's clients at double their original investment. The Federal Reserve would cover half the bill, the hedge fund community the balance. They'd call it a 'regulatory fee' and as long as everyone had to pay, no fund would lose their standing. The arrangements were finished in minutes.

"Henrik, would you wait with Jason until his car returns?" Zeki walked me to the door and spoke quietly as he handed me a business card. "Larry is a friend and a very good lawyer. He will charge you a fortune, and it will be worth it." He turned back to Henrik. "And would you ask Mr. Smalls to join us? We would like to finish this up and see him on his way. It is almost time for dinner."

Henrik and I left the room and reentered the cacophony of the party. The noise level was louder than ever. Henrik guided me toward the front door. The scent of grilled prime beef overwhelmed the cigar haze.

"Henrik, it's a long ride back to Manhattan. Do you think I could get a couple of those lobster rolls to go?"

LOBSTER MACARONI SALAD

INGREDIENTS

- 2 pounds cooked fresh lobster meat
- 1 lb. elbow macaroni
- 3 stalks celery
- 1 medium onion
- 1 cup mayonnaise
- 1 tsp. salt
- ½ tsp. pepper
- 5 hard-boiled eggs
- Paprika

DIRECTIONS

Cook macaroni until soft. Drain and rinse with cold water. Pat dry. In large mixing bowl add macaroni. Add salt and pepper. Finely dice celery and onion. Shred lobster meat with your fingertips. Gently mix in. Then fold in mayo with large spatula. Taste and adjust if needed. Cover and chill before serving. Put in serving bowl. Top with sliced eggs and paprika for garnish.

Entrée

Circle of Life

BY KRISTI BELCAMINO

IT WAS THE first time Delia had killed.

He'd fought so hard. She would never until the day she died forget the desperate look he gave her as the life seeped out of him, until his beady black eyes were deadened, the light extinguished forever.

In her kitchen, Delia stared at her blood-covered hands as she ran them under scalding water.

Her hands seemed alien, foreign, like something detached from her. It seemed as if she were cleaning up someone else's mess, watching from afar. She had to remind herself that the sticky, bloody hands in the sink in front of her were attached to her body. Slowly, her skin emerged as the blood washed off her hands and the sink basin filled with frothy pink bubbles.

Wiping her hands off on a clean towel, she began sharpening her largest butcher knife.

Still, she couldn't stop staring at her hands. They looked clean and fresh. Nobody would ever guess that they were the hands of a murderer.

It was odd. She thought she'd feel more. She thought she'd feel horror or sadness or guilt. But there was nothing. Nothing. She'd made it into something much more feared and awful than the actual act entailed.

Now she understood how serial killers could live with themselves. It wasn't that big a deal. You could turn a switch and shut off that part of your brain.

It became very clinical and medical—death was part of the circle of life, after all.

She had to remind herself that it was her own bare hands that had squeezed the life out of Thomas. And once he was dead, she'd cut off his head. That'd been the messy part. Luckily, she'd worn an apron. But still. Oh God. So much blood.

The fucker deserved it, though.

He'd been taunting her for months. He'd invaded her home and taken over.

He was there first thing in the morning and there when she went to bed at night. But worse than that, he'd come between her and her husband. She longed for a time when Thomas wasn't in their life.

From the first minute they had met, she could tell Thomas hated her. And she hated him right back.

Cliff told her to give it time. She would grow to love Thomas and see his value in their household.

"Having him here is going to save us money. I promise. Give him a chance."

"Never," she'd spit out, eyes furious. It was Cliff's fault that her peaceful life had been invaded. She glanced at the clock; Cliff would be home from work in three hours.

She needed to get to work.

Most of the mess outside had been cleaned up. She'd sprinkled hay on the blood that remained.

Sighing, she grabbed her butcher knife and began digging into Thomas's bowels.

She would make the best meal they'd had in months. She had all the right spices and herbs and would even make a batch of her famous mashed potatoes to go with it. The gravy the meat would provide would be divine.

Cliff would ask for seconds. She smiled. For sure.

· · · · ·

The knife was sharp, but the guts were a little messy. Setting down the knife, she hunted in her basement pantry until she found an old box of latex gloves she had once bought to deal with slicing jalapenos.

Grabbing some plastic trash bags, she spread them across the dining room table, and then across the floor to catch anything that seeped off the cutting board onto the ground.

She pulled the gloves on and slopped a handful of bloody mess into her nearby trash can. She gagged a little.

Better not vomit. That would ruin dinner for sure.

Good God. She'd no idea that preparing the dead meat would be the worst part. She thought the killing would be the hardest.

For the next two hours, she cleaned and chopped and braised and simmered. Testing a bite here and there to make sure she got the flavors right.

The smell of something yummy roasting had begun to fill the house when Cliff pulled into the driveway. Shit. He was early. Way too early. She'd wanted to surprise him. She'd wanted everything to be perfect.

She looked down with dismay at the blood on her apron and the mess protruding from her trash can. Quickly, she ripped off her rubber gloves and threw them in the trash. Then she untied the apron and threw it down the laundry chute. She tied and bagged the trash, throwing it out the back door.

By the time he walked in to the kitchen, she had re-applied her lipstick and was scrubbing the kitchen sink, working on making the stainless steel gleam.

He leaned over and kissed her. "Wow, something smells amazing. What's for dinner?"

"You're early. I was hoping to surprise you."

He looked at her, tilting his head.

"Something about you is different. I can't tell what it is. It's like you are glowing. What did you do today?"

"You'll see. It's not quite ready," she said smiling.

"It smells wonderful. Can you at least give me a hint what's on the menu?"

She smiled, leaning back against the sink. "How about you guess?"

"A roast?"

"Nope."

"Pork chops."

"Nuh uh."

"Lasagna!"

"Not even close."

"Meatloaf?"

"No, silly."

"Well, whatever it is, I'm sure it's going to taste delicious."

She leaned over and kissed him long and hard on the lips. When she drew back, she said, "Oh trust me, it's going to be the best meal ever."

"Wonderful."

He hadn't brought up the fact that it was the first time she'd cooked for him for more than two months. It had been her own silent protest against Thomas. He knew it. She knew it. But neither one of them had mentioned it.

"Well, I can't wait." He rubbed his hands together.

"Why don't you go get changed into something comfortable," she said. "We can have an aperitif before we eat. Dinner won't be ready for another hour."

"Boy, did I luck out in the wife department. That sounds great. Meet you back here in a few." He left the room.

Very carefully, she made them each a gin and tonic, being sure to squeeze fresh lime on the ice cubes before she added the gin and tonic to the tumblers.

Making drinks felt normal.

Like it had before. Before Thomas wedged himself into their marriage.

They would survive.

It could happen. They could return to their old lives. The way it was before Thomas.

Cliff hadn't even asked about Thomas. That was the first sign that she had done the right thing. Tonight was just the start.

For the first time in weeks, she felt hopeful.

Today's violence had been necessary. She wasn't going to share her husband with anyone or anything. He was all hers. She'd seen how Cliff looked at Thomas. She wasn't stupid. Her husband had loved him.

At first it had shocked her. How could Cliff love that ugly face? But he did. She'd come up on them once when they didn't notice. Cliff had been caressing and sweet talking Thomas. She'd snuck away before they noticed. Huddled on the floor of the bathroom, she'd nearly thrown up. Her insides turned red with rage.

It had taken her a month to figure out what to do. There was no other way.

Thomas had to die.

Then Cliff would see how serious she was about their marriage.

Sure, at first when she told him, he'd be mad. But he'd get over it. After dinner, she'd take him into the bedroom and fuck his brains out.

He'd never think about Thomas again.

Sure, after ten years of marriage, it was to be expected that some of the flame had fizzled. But Cliff's behavior was unacceptable.

She'd realized that when she heard Cliff talking to Thomas in that sweet voice. It had been years since he'd used that tone with her.

With Thomas gone, all that sweet talk would be directed at her.

She'd be the best wife ever. He didn't need Thomas. Thomas didn't have a pussy.

She'd be the kind of wife he needed. The kind of wife he wanted. He wouldn't have to ever look for love somewhere else again.

Cliff had drained his drink and the sun was beginning to set when the oven timer went off.

She stood. "Go wash your hands and freshen up. I'll have dinner on the table shortly."

In the kitchen, she took down her fanciest plates, the ones Cliff's mother had given them for a wedding present. Her hands shook as she lifted the huge baking dish out of the oven. Carefully, she sliced off a tiny piece of meat, stabbed it with a fork, and put it in her mouth. At first she moved the piece around on her tongue, letting the flavors soak in.

Yum! Gently, slowly, she put her teeth on it. For a second her forehead crinkled. Was it too tough? But then she bit down and the juices flowed into her mouth. Mmmm. Perfect.

She took the silver tongs and lifted the choicest cut of meat, laying it lovingly on Cliff's plate.

"It smells fantastic. Do you need any help in there?" Cliff's voice was a mixture of anticipation and happiness. He was pleased.

"No, but thank you. I think I have this. You could do something for me, though? Will you turn off the overhead lights, light some candles, and pour us some wine? There's a new bottle of red on the sideboard."

"Will do."

She wanted him good and drunk when she explained that the meat they were eating was actually Thomas. It would make it more palatable.

Finally, she had prepared two plates perfectly. Well, nearly perfectly. One more small thing: she dug in the refrigerator and found a few pieces of parsley and small red tomatoes that she placed lovingly around the edges. Stepping back, she beamed with pride.

Beautiful.

She held the plates in front of her and proudly walked into the dining room. In the candlelight, she saw Cliff's face glow. He was smiling at her until she placed the plate in front of him.

"Try it?" She was still a little nervous that it wouldn't taste okay, that he wouldn't like it.

She watched anxiously as he took his fork and knife and sliced a morsel from a breast piece. "Oh, I can already tell it is so tender."

Then he put a piece in his mouth and chewed slowly with his eyes closed. She waited, wringing her hands, until he swallowed and opened his eyes.

He gave her a look she would treasure forever.

"It's perfect. The most perfect roasted chicken I've ever tasted."

"It's not chicken."

His eyebrows drew together in confusion. "What? It's not chicken?" He examined the piece of meat on his fork, head tilted.

That's when she plastered the largest, fakest smile she'd ever worn in her life onto her face and said defiantly. "Nope. Rooster."

Cliff stood so suddenly that his chair tipped over behind him, his face ashen as he turned toward the window facing the chicken coop.

"Nooooo!" He sounded wounded. "What have you done? Delia? What have you done?"

Hearing his tone, the hurt in his voice just proved she had done the right thing.

"He was coming between us, Cliff. It was him or me. I saw how you look at him. I've heard you talking to him whispering sweet nothings. I know you love him more than me. I won't stand for it anymore!" A little spittle came out of her mouth as she shouted.

Taking her napkin, she tried to compose herself, eloquently wiping her chin.

Cliff's face had gone from white to bright red. The veins on his neck were bulging. He held his hands in fists clenched at his sides.

"You? What? You're crazy. I knew you were going off the deep end lately, but you've surpassed any sort of wackiness I could've imagined. You're goddamn crazy. Goddamn loony tunes. I can't believe I'm married to a total cuckoo nutcase."

At that moment, Delia's heart grew black.

Clamping her lips together, she watched as his fingers pried open the blinds, his head against the glass, searching in the dark for his beloved pet. Then his grip loosened and he collapsed onto the floor under the window, clutching at his chest and gasping. She thought for a minute about getting up and going to him.

Then decided against it.

He'd made his bed. Now he could lie in it. He had betrayed her. Even in his last moments. Even in death, he loved Thomas more than her. He had proven it.

She watched his body twitch, drool coming out of his mouth. Then he grew still.

Slowly, she took her knife and fork and delicately cut off another small piece of the meat, dipping it delicately in the gravy before she placed it on her tongue. She sat there savoring the flavors and tenderness. The meat practically melted in her mouth.

She sat there, sipping wine and eating her dinner, until the candles burned down to the wick and flickered out. The entire room grew dark.

KYATCHI'S HOT DOGS

Courtesy of Sam Peterson, owner (www.kyatchi.com)

- **The House Dog:** Grilled shisito peppers and a house-made mix of yuzu paste and Japanese mayonnaise.
- **Yakisoba Dog:** Soba noodles stir fried with onions, oil, and soy sauce. Topped with pickled red ginger and Japanese mayonnaise.
- **Avacado and Egg Dog:** Chopped hard-boiled egg mixed with Japanese mayonnaise and topped with slices of avocado.
- **Kimchi Dog:** Kimchi topped with a mix of sesame oil and Japanese mayonnaise.

Our hot dogs are made to order by Peterson Craftsman Beef from Osceola, WI. They are made with grass-fed beef and have no preservatives (nitrates) in them. They are made with real pork casings as well.

Wolfie

BY CHRISTINE HUSOM

THE FIRST THING that registered in Tara's waking mind was that the sliver of light shining through the one-inch gap in her bedroom curtains meant she had lived to see another day. The second thing was she had been forced out of her sleep—pulled from a heavenly dream—because something was crawling on her bare arm. Her breath caught in her throat. She knew what it was before she glimpsed at it. With sheer strength of will, she brushed the hairy wolf spider off and rolled out of bed onto the floor, taking her pillow with her. It felt like every ounce of energy had drained from her body. She could barely rise up on her hands and knees and crawl away.

Tara reached the corner of her bedroom and sat down, scooting her butt to the wall. She drew up her knees, leaned her chest against her thighs, and wrapped her arms around the calves of her legs. She rocked back and forth, not allowing herself to scream bloody murder at the top of her lungs like the first time, and too many times since, because an eight-legged critter was planted on her sleeping body. Her husband would not have the satisfaction of hearing her shriek.

Not ever again. He'd used her phobia against her once too often. Tara brought the pillow to her face, muffling her voice as moans from deep within her spilled into the cushioned padding.

Spiders were the only thing in life she feared more than her husband. And her husband was the only thing in life she hated more than spiders. She'd given up analyzing why he'd chosen her as a secret target of his sadism, or how he had hidden his true character from her before they married. He was popular and well-liked by scores of people who didn't know the real Kelvin. He was the CEO of a healthcare company, and contributed beaucoup bucks to charities.

And he made certain everyone knew it, too.

When he began pursuing her the year before, Tara was stunned. Women were lined up, vying for a chance with the most desired widower in the city. But she wasn't one of them. She was not in the same, or even related, social circle as Kelvin. Although Tara personally didn't give a hoot about status, he was way out of her league.

The people he socialized with were clueless about who the real Kelvin was. He'd manipulated them into believing he was a kind, generous man who lovingly doted on his wife, evidenced in part by the breathtaking amount of money he spent on gifts for her. He cleverly presented the treasures at gatherings with friends, always with a number of witnesses. As Kelvin clasped a bracelet on her arm, or a necklace around her neck, or slipped a ring on her finger, it was her duty to appear awed, and forever grateful. The gasps and jealous mutters of others helped remind her she needed to perform well.

If she didn't play her part, she would pay the inevitable price. Kelvin had given Tara a demonstration of what that was shortly after they'd returned from their idyllic honeymoon. She could have fought back, and likely won, but she knew it would only make things worse. She'd been plotting her escape ever since.

A day or two after his public gift presentations, he would return them as a way to penalize her. The irony of it all: Tara was relieved when he did. She felt it was immoral to spend that kind of money on jewelry, especially on pieces she would not want to wear. But she kept that to herself. Why make things worse?

As she'd dug deep into Kelvin's secret dealings, she was surprised he was still alive. He had blackmailed some high rollers, and she had no idea how he'd gotten away with it. It was probably a question of time before someone ordered a hit on him, but she couldn't worry about that.

Tara tightened the hold on her calves and braved another look at the wolf spider slowly making its way across the embroidered pearl white bedspread. Chills danced up her spine, and goose bumps sprouted on her arms and legs as she shuddered. After Kelvin planted the first wolf spider on her sleeping body, she had forced herself to do some research on them. This one was brownish gray, and over an inch long. It had hair on its legs and belly, and claws at the end of its legs. It had three rows of eyes; four small ones in the first row, two medium-size ones in the third, and two huge ones front and center in the second.

Was there a creepier crawling creature anywhere in the world? From time to time, Tara looked up spiders on the Internet, making every effort to desensitize herself, to calm her fears and overcome her phobia. But the terror continued.

She was too young to remember the incident that had started the paralyzing fear.

According to her mother, she'd been playing with toys on her living room floor when a spider crawled out from somewhere and bit her. There was no venom to make her sick, but she'd cried, "Owie, owie, owie," for a long time from the painful bite. And her biggest fear, her only phobia, wormed its way into her life.

On one of their first dates, Kelvin had coaxed her to tell him about the most terrible thing that had ever happened to her, her worst memory. The question struck her as odd at that stage in their relationship, but Kelvin wasn't like most men she knew. She shrugged off her concern and made the mistake of relating the spider story. What she didn't know at the time was he was looking for a confession to a crime she'd been involved with, something she went to great lengths to hide.

Tara heard Kelvin walking down the long hallway toward the bedroom and jumped up.

She darted into the bathroom, quietly closed the door, then turned on the shower and was out of her nightgown and in the tub before Kelvin opened the bathroom door.

"Why are you taking a shower?" he called to her.

To hide from you. To wash the footprints of a hairy spider from my skin. To cleanse my body and clear my mind.

When she didn't answer immediately, Kelvin yanked open one of the glass enclosures.

Tara sucked in a quick breath so she wouldn't gasp. Her body tensed more tightly still, but she gained control of her voice and calmly answered, "Oh, Kelvin. You're still home?"

"I asked why you're taking a shower." Because she always took baths.

"I was too tired to bathe last night." *Or not.*

Kelvin let out a hearty, wicked laugh. "It wasn't the little something that joined you in bed this morning?"

Her strong sense of pride made it easy to fib as she scrubbed away with the soapy loofah. "What are you talking about?"

His eyes darkened and his jaw locked. Then he slammed the door and spit out, "Bitch."

Tara squeezed her eyes shut and braced herself for the spray of shattered glass she expected, but the door remained intact. Surprisingly.

She turned the dial on the shower head to Massage, and as the water pulsated over her tight shoulder muscles, she knew the day had come to end her misery. *Massage. It had to work.*

Tara got out of the shower, dressed quickly, then went to the kitchen for a container. She sifted through the cupboard full of plastic food storage bowls and smiled when she found the one she was looking for. It had a vegetable drainer cover. Next she hunted for bait, and a dead house fly on the living room window ledge fit the bill to a tee. She pushed it into the bowl, then returned to the scene of the assault.

The spider was on the carpet, heading toward the bathroom. She'd have sooner walked on a bed of hot coals, but the anger that rocked her very soul propelled her toward the creature. Tara set the bowl on its side, in the spider's path, and it crawled into the bowl, claiming its snack. Tara snapped on the cover and picked up the bowl. "Wolfie, you've got a very important job ahead of you. You're going to be my evidence and my alibi." She held the bowl with her arms extended as far away from her face as possible and carried it to the kitchen. She found a spot in the cabinet under the sink, set the bowl with her captive on a shelf, and closed the door.

Tara made a cup of coffee, and as she settled onto a counter stool, questions that had haunted her for twenty years played in her mind. *Have you ever been arrested? Have you ever been convicted of a crime?* Hot waves of shame washed through her. She had rationalized, convinced herself, that technically the answer to both questions was no. And that's what she put on her first public sector job application, and her second, and her third. After she'd successfully landed the third position, she knew it was the perfect fit. She worked her way to the top from there.

Kelvin refused to disclose how he had uncovered the criminal incident she so carefully buried. It was part of his power trip. Maybe someday she'd figure it out, but that wasn't important. The critical issue was no one in the city or county or state ever found out. The scandal would negate the long list of positive things she'd done. All the people she'd mentored, helped, and saved would be forgotten. Her stellar career would be cloaked with a shroud of mistrust and betrayal.

Tara watched the long hand on the clock move to the next minute. Time marched on. But not always fast enough. Four o'clock, the hour when Kelvin normally returned from wherever he spent the bulk of his Saturday, seemed like an eternity away. But from four until six, his schedule at home was routine. He would drink a tall glass of wine, then head into his fitness center for an hour-long in-home massage by his therapist. That always put him to sleep for at least a half hour. And he slept like the dead. *Like the dead.* Thinking about the sinister simile put a smile on her face.

Tara was too keyed up to hang around the house. Plus, she didn't want to face Kelvin and another confrontation when he got home. Not to mention the fact that Wolfie the spider was holed up in the cupboard under her sink, and that added another layer of stress.

She drove to her office and tried to concentrate on getting through the never-ending pile of paperwork. Instead, her mind kept drifting to a plan she'd concocted one night when she couldn't sleep. Her escape plan. She leaned back in her chair and closed her eyes. When she opened them again, she spotted a common house spider on her office window. It was outside and she was safe, but she trembled anyway. Tara had embarrassed herself more than a few times with her staff, calling them into her office to get rid of spiders. She wouldn't be surprised if they joked about it behind her back, but she didn't care.

The hours slowly passed. At 4:15, Tara drew in a long breath through her mouth and let it out slowly through her nostrils. Then she picked up her cell phone and typed a text message to Kelvin: "I'll be home soon with groceries for one of your favorite dinners. Have a relaxing massage." She didn't expect a reply because he'd be on the massage table by then. But it was the last message she would send him. She locked up the office, drove to the market, and bought the needed items.

When Tara arrived home, she backed her car into the garage, turned the ignition off, and sat for a minute looking at the other three vehicles in there: a classic 1971 Lamborghini, a silver Lexus, and a brand spanking new Mercedes Benz SUV. Kelvin always backed the vehicles in, and she followed suit. As it so happened, that would play nicely in her plan.

She was about to walk away from all the luxuries of living in an elegant, much-too-big house. It would be a dream come true, going back to a simpler life where the bulk of her pressures came from her job, not an evil husband. She gathered up her shopping bag and pushed the button that closed the garage door.

Tara was at her stove preparing shrimp and artichokes in wine, thinking about her involvement in a crime that had come back to haunt her in the worst way. She was barely eighteen, giving her boyfriend and one of his friends a ride home. Len asked her to stop at a gas station so he could grab some smokes. The two boys went in and she stayed in the car, listening to music. A few minutes later, they ran back to the car and yelled at her to drive away. Fast. She sped off, asking Len what it was all about, but all he did was shake his head.

Later that night she saw it on the news. Len's and his friend's images had been caught on camera committing a heinous crime. Their faces weren't visible, but she easily identified them.

When she saw Len's friend pull out a gun and shoot the clerk, she almost threw up. According to the news report, they'd escaped in a blue four-door Ford Escort with an unknown license plate.

Tara had called the sheriff's office right away and told the deputy everything she knew.

They interviewed her for hours and the county attorney wanted to throw the book at her, charge her with second-degree murder. But in the end, she was offered a plea deal. Humiliation and guilt drove her to bury the truth. She should have been straightforward about it from the get-go because the more time that passed, the more deceitful it seemed. She left her home state and started a new life in Minnesota, pursuing the career she'd always wanted.

Tara was lost in thought when Brett, the beefy massage therapist, cleared his throat behind her. She startled, then turned to greet him.

"Ah, sorry, I didn't mean give you a scare."

"No worries. I guess I was concentrating on my cooking, didn't hear you."

The therapist nodded. "That sure smells good."

"It's one of Kelvin's favorites."

"He is one lucky man."

She smiled. "Thanks."

"We'll see you next week."

"See ya."

As soon as Brett was gone, via the side door in the kitchen, Tara turned the burners to low and put covers on the two pans. She scooted into the large room Kelvin used as a fitness center. He'd had it sealed tighter than a drum to keep his workout noises inside. He had equipment many gyms could not afford. The blinds were drawn, and there was a small diffuser filling the area with the soothing scent of lavender oil. The massage table was close to the door that led to the garage. Kelvin was lying on his stomach, his head supported by the table's cradle, snoring away.

Tara quietly slipped into the garage, pulling the door shut behind her.

She climbed into the Lamborghini and started the engine. It purred like a kitten. She eased the door closed without slamming it and then did the same with the Lexus SUV. She drew in a big breath and held it as she hurried back to the fitness center. She left the door open to the garage. Kelvin hadn't stirred, as far as she could tell. She needed a breath, and as she left the room as she let out a lungful of air. "Whoooo."

How long will it take? Tara knew that older vehicles emitted a much higher concentration of carbon monoxide, and was glad the Lamborghini was parked closest to the fitness center. With the two vehicles running, she figured it would be over in fifteen minutes. The dangerous thing about CO was that even if there was oxygen in an enclosed space, carbon monoxide prevented hemoglobin from delivering oxygen to the body.

Tara was fairly confident little CO would seep into the rest of the house, but she went outside to the back yard just in case. It was a breezy, late spring day. She wandered around, looking at the tulips and grape hyacinth blooms and wondered how everything had gone so wrong in her life. She had talked with countless abused women through the years and pondered again and again why they stayed, why they didn't leave. But Tara now knew from firsthand experience one of the main reasons: you can run, but you can't hide. To really escape, she had to eliminate the threat. It was basic survival.

After the longest twenty minutes of her life, Tara went back into the house then out the kitchen door that led to the garage. She pushed the button to open the overhead door, then quickly turned off the car engines before returning inside. She opened windows, upstairs and down, before braving a look in the fitness center. Kelvin was still face down on the table, his arms at his side.

She went back into the house and moved as fast as possible, turning on the ceiling fan and the two fans that were mounted on the wall. Then she ran out again. She checked the four CO detectors in the house, and none of them showed elevated levels. She unplugged one of them, carried it to the fitness center, and plugged it in there. Its loud beep made her jump and speeded up the adrenaline coursing through her body. What was she doing? What had she done?

It took time, but the fourth time she looked, the detector was silent and the CO level was at zero. She checked the level in the garage, and it was clear, too. Over the next minutes, she closed all but a couple of the windows and lowered the garage door.

It was time to see if Kelvin was dead or alive. She gingerly made her way to the table, half-fearing he was asleep and would wake up with bad headache. She put her hand on his back. He wasn't breathing. She checked for a pulse. No pulse. Tara hurried into the kitchen, taking a quick look at the meal that would be tossed, and grabbed the bowl with Wolfie inside it from under the sink. He was still alive.

My new best friend. She carried him into the fitness center, opened the bowl, released Wolfie onto Kelvin's back, then ran to the kitchen and stuck the bowl in the dishwasher. When she returned, she dialed 911. She was out of breath and sounded distressed. "It's Tara Estrem. Send help. I think my husband's had a heart attack. I can't find a pulse."

"Oh my God, Chief Estrem. Have you started CPR?"

"No, I need help rolling him off the massage table."

"Hang on. Rescue is on the way, and two of your police officers will be close behind."

"Tell them to come in through the garage. And hurry." She hung up, then opened the overhead door once more. The sound of sirens got closer and closer then stopped. Two first responders and Officers Wallen and Larson rushed in.

The officers both shot their boss a sympathetic look. Officer Wallen shook his head when he spotted the spider on Kelvin's back, flicked it off, and stomped on it. The responders and officers worked as a team, turning Kelvin onto his back. They checked his breathing and circulation, and performed CPR for six futile minutes before they called it.

Tara had moved to the back of the room and was sitting on a weight-lifting bench. Officer Larson joined her and wrapped an arm around her shoulder. "I'm so sorry, boss. We were too late."

Tara nodded and lifted tear-filled eyes to one of her brightest recruits. "You tried."

"I'm so sorry. And with your spider phobia, seeing that big ugly thing on Kelvin's back must have made it even worse."

Tara shrugged. Wolfie was creepy, no doubt. But if the question of carbon monoxide ever came up, he'd be the evidence she needed to disavow that theory. A creature that small would die long before a 250-pound man.

SHRIMP AND ARTICHOKES IN WINE

INGREDIENTS

- 6 oz. package long grain and wild rice
- 8 oz. fresh sliced mushrooms
- ¼ cup butter
- 3 tablespoons butter
- Additional butter, if needed
- ½ teaspoon salt, if desired
- ¾ cup cream
- 12 oz. frozen cooked shrimp
- 7 oz. jar of marinated artichoke hearts, drained
- ¼ cup dry white wine
- ¼ cup grated parmesan cheese

DIRECTIONS

Prepare rice as directed on package. While rice is cooking, sauté mushrooms in butter until tender, 3 to 4 minutes. Remove mushrooms with a slotted spoon; reserve. Stir flour and salt into butter (add more, if needed). Cook, stirring with a wire whip, until smooth and bubbling. Mixture will be quite thick. Add shrimp and artichokes and heat about 5 minutes until mixture is hot. Stir in mushrooms, wine, and parmesan cheese. Simmer a few minutes. Serve over rice. Makes 4 to 6 servings.

Note: This recipe works well substituting chicken for the shrimp.

Love, Lobster, and Lies

BY NANCY TESLER

I RAN INTO Phyllis Lutz standing in line at the American Airlines ticket counter in Philadelphia. I arrived there out of breath and thoroughly out of sorts after a marathon sprint across the terminal to the departure gate, where I was informed that I'd just missed my connecting flight to Newark.

Phyllis was a former client with whom I hadn't parted on the best of terms, so seeing her didn't exactly make my rapidly deteriorating day. A couple of years ago she'd come to my office complaining of stomachaches and migraines, the genesis of which I came to believe was her professor husband's inability to make enough money to allow her access to the social circles to which she aspired. As a biofeedback therapist, my job is to help my clients gain control over their internal responses to pain and stress. I do this by teaching, among other things, deep breathing, relaxation, and visualization exercises. It's a kind of "heal thyself" alternative to the conventional medical approach. Phyllis regarded the techniques I employ as something akin to voodoo. She terminated our sessions quite publicly the day my name appeared in our local supermarket tabloid as the prime suspect in the murder of my soon-to-be-ex-husband's soon-to-be fiancée.

Phyllis was on my flight from San Francisco, where I'd gone to speak at a biofeedback seminar, but I hadn't seen her either in the airport or on the plane. I almost didn't recognize her.

She'd lost quite a bit of weight below the waist, swapping it for a pair of surgically enhanced D-cups above. It was a winning redistribution. She was also now a carefully made-up honey-blonde. We exchanged polite hellos and I complimented her on her transformation.

"I heard you've made some changes in your life too, Carrie," she said, as we waited for the line to move. "I'm told you actually married that cop. What was his name again?"

I don't know which I resented more, the emphasis on that cop or the word "actually."

"Brodsky," I replied shortly. "Lieutenant Ted Brodsky." Ted's the homicide detective who headed the investigation of the murder I mentioned earlier. Things did not go well with us initially, mainly because I'd been spotted spying on my husband's young playmate draped, half-nude but very much alive, on my favorite chaise lounge. Unfortunately for me (not to mention for her), that was the day she was conked over the head and tossed into my former swimming pool.

"Wasn't he just a sergeant when you were accused of—"

"He was promoted."

"Oh." She giggled. "I hope it came with a pay raise."

I took a deep cleansing breath, just as I teach my clients to do when they're in a "fight-or-flight" situation.

"Come on, Carrie, I only meant your ex is so damned rich. Don't you miss the lifestyle?"

"No."

"Did you take his name? The cop?"

"I still use Carlin professionally."

"Doesn't he mind? He struck me as—well, you know, the macho type."

"He's got a strong ego. He's handling it."

I was spared further interrogation by our arrival at the counter. The airline rep informed us it would be impossible to get anyone on a plane to Newark until the following day, adding that we'd be lucky to get on a flight even then. Phyllis made a huge fuss and the harassed rep finally gave her a voucher for a hotel. I was considering renting a car and driving home, even though it's a two-and-a-half-hour trip to Norwood, NJ, where I live with my teenage son and daughter, our four animals, and my wonderful, sexy new husband. But I deep-sixed the idea because it was past ten, I'd been up since half past five, and I was exhausted. I turned back to the rep. "I'd like a hotel voucher too, please."

"Sorry, I just gave this lady the last one I had," the rep said. "You could try calling some of the hotels yourself, but there are a bunch of conventions in town and I'm told most of them are booked."

My stress level went into orbit as I pictured myself scrunched up on a lumpy chair in the airport lounge with an overweight snorer on one side and a leering would-be rapist on the other.

Phyllis smirked as she took in my expression. "Remember, now, Carrie. This is not a life-threatening situation." (A mocking reference to the mantra I teach my clients so they keep things in perspective when they run into the modern equivalent of a Tyrannosaurus Rex.) I wanted to punch her. Sometimes it's just not possible to practice what you preach.

"Why don't you and your friend share the room?" the rep inquired brightly.

"Oh no, that's not . . ."

"I suppose we could," Phyllis said, surprising me. "We could rent a car and drive home tomorrow."

I hesitated, contemplating my options—a long drive tonight in the dark, spend the night on that lumpy chair in the airport, or put up with Phyllis's company but receive a comfortable bed as a reward. The bed won, but not by much. And I had to admit, it was nice of Phyllis considering that not so long ago, in her head, she'd had my face on every post office wall in the country. So I accepted and texted Ted that I'd be staying in a hotel overnight and driving home in the morning.

"How're the headaches?" I asked, making an attempt at conversation as we headed for the exit.

"It certainly wasn't anything you did, but they're mostly gone."

If I knew how to gnash my teeth I would have gnashed. "I assume the stomachaches are better as well?"

"Pretty much. I'm very careful what I eat now."

"Happy to hear it." I changed the subject. "I'm really glad I put all my things in this carry-on. God knows where our suitcases could have ended up."

Phyllis grimaced. "I wasn't as lucky as you. The St. John I was going to wear tomorrow will probably make it to Newark next week, or maybe never."

St. John? Professor Greg must have hit the lottery!

And then, casually, she threw out, "I have an appointment with my publisher. I hate to be wearing this old thing when I meet him." She indicated her gorgeous red cashmere sweater.

"You're getting a book published?"

"I have an advance for a cookbook. I won a cooking contest with my recipe for lobster flambé in whiskey, and the first prize was a publishing contract."

"Wow," I said, wondering if she'd blown the whole advance on the St. John. "That's awesome." *Why am I talking like my fifteen-year-old daughter?* "I didn't know you were a gourmet cook. You never mentioned it. "

A taxi pulled up, and it was a few minutes until we settled ourselves inside. Phyllis gave the cabbie the name of the hotel, then turned to me. "I'm not. Greg always did the cooking. About the only thing he ever did well. The lobster recipe was in his file."

Greg was gone? Maybe she'd killed him for his recipe file. I hadn't read his obituary anywhere. But then, I don't usually read obits.

I was reluctant to ask. Wearing red, she didn't look to be in mourning, so maybe his exit was old news. "I'm sorry," I murmured, not sure what I was sorry for.

She waved her hand dismissively as if we'd been talking about an annoying employee she'd had to let go. "There's the possibility of a TV show."

"No kidding!"

"The competition was fierce. You wouldn't believe how those other contestants reacted when I won. Some of them were absolutely cutthroat. I had to guard my recipe with my life."

Had I misjudged the woman? I was having a hard time believing she could concentrate on anything beyond her wardrobe and her social aspirations. "Hey, you could be looking at really big bucks."

"I guess." She fluffed her hair. "When I set my mind on something, I don't let anything stop me. It's how I am."

I wondered how she'd gotten to be a participant in this contest. She'd just admitted she didn't cook. Before I could form a question, she suddenly pressed her hands against her forehead. "Oh God. Maybe it's seeing you, but I think I feel a headache coming on."

"You've been under a lot of pressure," I said, soothingly. "You'll be okay once you get a good night's sleep."

She glared at me. "How can I sleep when I have a headache? When we get to the hotel I'm going to have a stiff drink in the bar."

"I don't think that's the best thing for—"

"Well, if it doesn't work you can try some of your voodoo on me when I get back to the room."

Gnash! "Sure. I'll be happy to if I'm still awake."

I remembered trying to warm those icicles she calls hands with guided imagery, a good exercise for migraine sufferers. Hot lava, steaming vapor, the fires of hell—nothing worked. I'd end up with sweaty palms and she'd leave my office with extremities frostier than when she arrived.

I never got a chance to try. I was asleep when my head hit the pillow, and when I woke in the morning the bed next to mine was empty.

I dressed quickly and checked the hotel restaurant, figuring Phyllis had awakened early and gone down for breakfast. No luck. I tried the restroom and the lobby. Maybe she'd gone for a walk to work off nervous energy. After all, this was a big day for her. Fortifying myself with a cup of coffee and a Danish, I pulled out my iPhone and checked to see if I still had her number in my contacts. Not there. I must have deleted her after that encounter in the supermarket. I headed for the reception desk.

"Has Mrs. Lutz checked out of Room 314?" I asked the young desk clerk.

He checked his computer. "No, Ma'am."

"Did she by any chance leave the voucher the airline gave us for the room?"

"No, Ma'am."

Great. Now I was stuck for the room bill as well as the car. I handed the clerk my credit card. "I'd like to check out now. Please cancel this if Mrs. Lutz comes back with the voucher." I scribbled a note telling her I couldn't wait any longer, signed the receipt, and went to check the room one last time. The bedspread was still on the bed as though she hadn't bothered getting under the covers. *Probably had a few too many,* I thought meanly. I grabbed my carry-on, left several dollars for the maid, and closed the door behind me. So much for Phyllis Lutz, the TV star. I was done with her, and good riddance. Phyllis Lutz was out of my life forever.

Wrong.

A couple of days later, I was in my office at my computer typing up notes when I got a text from Ted.

"Call me when you have a break between clients."

I glanced at my watch, picked up my cell and hit "Ted." It was a little before twelve. Maybe I was about to get an invitation to lunch.

He answered on the first ring. "Carrie, didn't you tell me you shared a room in Philly with that Lutz woman but drove home without her?

"Yeah, she left before I was up and stuck me with the bill."

"Well, apparently she never came home. Her husband's filed a missing persons report."

"Her husband. I thought he was dead."

A pause. "He doesn't seem to be aware of that."

"Well, she didn't actually say what happened to him, but she referred to him in the past tense so I assumed at least they're not together."

"It seems he didn't get that message either, and he's worried sick." He cleared his throat.

"Uh, listen, honey, apparently you were the last person to see her before she disappeared. A couple of Philadelphia's finest are on their way here to talk to you. I thought I'd bring them by. When's your last client?

I'll try to hold them off until you finish."

• • • • •

"I don't understand. This woman wasn't a friend of yours, but you shared a hotel room."

We were in my office, I in my safe space behind my desk, the two Philadelphia detectives in my client chairs opposite me, and Ted sitting on the loveseat facing my double monitor computer set-up. The balding middle-aged detective who was grilling me had introduced himself as Sergeant Frazier. His manner was pleasant, but he kept asking the same questions in different ways, hoping, I knew from experience, to catch me in a lie. This was feeling way too familiar.

"Why wouldn't you have gotten your own room?"

"There were a bunch of conventions in town. The hotels were booked. I was very tired and it made sense at—"

The other detective interrupted. His name was Morelli; he was linebacker huge and if Ted hadn't been there I think he would've been playing bad cop. As it was, he didn't sound particularly friendly. "Are you telling us Mrs. Lutz got up in the morning, used the bathroom, got dressed, opened and closed the door to your room, and you never heard a thing?"

I glanced at Ted who, reluctant to interfere with another jurisdiction's investigation, hadn't said a word so far. He nodded at me as if to say, *Just tell the truth.*

"It was after eleven by the time we checked in. I was dead on my feet. She went to the bar to have a nightcap but I went right to bed. I never heard a thing after I closed my eyes."

The detectives exchanged glances.

From Frazier. "Are you saying she never came back to the room?"

"I—I don't know. The bedspread was still on, but I assumed she'd been drinking and had fallen asleep on top of the covers."

From Morelli. "Are you aware the desk clerk never saw Mrs. Lutz leave?"

"I asked him if she'd checked out and he told me she hadn't. But certainly the bartender must remember her. Don't they have cameras in the hotel?"

"They're being checked. So what do you think happened to her?"

"I haven't a clue!" My fight or flight response kicked in. Maybe I was in a life-threatening situation and these guys were T-rexes. I certainly wasn't in a position to fight. Maybe it was time to flee. I pushed my chair back. "For God's sake, do you think I'm a witch and magically made her disappear? I haven't seen the woman in years. Why would I—"

"Carrie, chill." Ted shook his head reprovingly at me but unwound his long legs and stood. "Gentlemen," he said in a voice I recognized as his "end of discussion" tone, "I think my wife has told you everything she knows. We're done here."

As I got to my feet, I thought of something about which neither detective had asked.

"She told me she had an appointment with her publisher the next afternoon and it was very important to her. She wouldn't have—"

"Her publisher?" Frazier looked confused.

"She wouldn't have missed it. She said some of the other contestants were jealous— cutthroat was the word she used, when she won the contest. She said she had to guard her lobster recipe with her life. You should be talking to them."

"What are you talking about?" Morelli asked. "What contest?"

"She'd won a cooking competition. Didn't her husband tell you? That's why she was in San Francisco."

Ted frowned. "Carrie, when her husband came in to report her missing, he told me she went to San Francisco for a reunion with some college friends. The appointment she missed was with people at her church. They're publishing a cookbook and she had contributed a recipe."

· · · · ·

They discovered Phyllis's body several days later in the trunk of an abandoned car that had been parked off the highway near a Philadelphia sub-urb. Ted told me the news as gently as he could, but it totally shook me. She'd been strangled. The car was stripped and wiped clean. No finger-prints were found. I was off the hook because it strained credulity for anyone to believe that I, at five-three and 110 pounds, could have killed her while she slept, carried her body down the elevator and through the lobby, and stashed it in the trunk of a car that was parked miles away. In my mind, the prime suspect was going to be the husband, Greg.

"I'm sorry for him," I told Ted as we were getting ready for bed the night after the discovery. "The few times I met him I liked him. He seemed a decent guy. His life's going to become a nightmare."

"Don't assume he's top of the list."

"Oh no? You cops always look at the spouse first. Or the ex," I said pointedly. Given my history, I was relating to the situation in which Greg Lutz would find himself. "Frazier and Morelli will say he had a motive."

"Do you think he had a motive?"

I sat on the edge of the bed and began rubbing lotion on my hands. "She was a horrible woman and she was always putting him down, but that doesn't mean he killed her."

"No, it doesn't."

"I wanted to kill her myself a few times."

He laughed. "Like I told you once, there's a monster inside all of us . . ."

". . . but most of us keep our monsters caged," I quoted. "I know."

"So stop worrying about him. There'll be a thorough investigation. There's probably something on those cameras. "

"Maybe he has an alibi. After all, she was killed in Philadelphia. Even if she called him and told him where she was staying, that's a pretty long drive."

"Time of death will be a factor." He joined me on the bed, dropped his shoes, and peeled off his socks. "As I remember he's not a very big guy."

"Is that important?"

"It'll help to eliminate him. Whoever killed her did it with his bare hands. Frazier told me. Crime of passion."

I shuddered as I thought about Phyllis's last moments. I didn't like her, but I never would have wished that on her. "I'll bet she went off with some pervert she met in the bar."

"Entirely possible." He yawned and got into bed. "You think you could close the door and keep the menagerie out tonight?"

I went to the door, peeked out, and saw no lurking animals. "I think they're with the kids."

"Good." He lifted the covers. "Come on in."

I crawled into bed and snuggled against him. "I can't imagine what it would be like living with her."

"Maybe she had redeeming qualities. Maybe she was a tiger in bed." He growled and kissed the back of my neck. "Speaking of tigers . . ."

"She was obviously leaving him. Otherwise, why did she talk about him in the past tense?"

"Give it up, sweetheart. It's not your problem to solve. And, thank God, it's not mine."

His hands were moving on me now and I was starting to lose my train of thought. "But why did she lie to me about the cooking contest? I know she liked to make herself important but—"

"Shush up," he murmured. And I did as his mouth came down on mine.

Ted doesn't call me Curious Georgette for nothing. I have a history. The following day after my last client left, I pulled up my notes on Phyllis's sessions hoping to see if she'd ever mentioned having enemies. She'd done considerable moaning about doctors who had misdiagnosed her or didn't care enough to cure her, and there was lots of complaining about Greg—who she blamed for everything, including their being childless— but nothing about anyone that raised red flags. I decided to check out her Facebook page because, unless the killer was a stranger she'd met in the bar, it would have to have been someone she had called from the hotel.

The first thing I noticed was that she had 1,421 "friends." *Yikes!* I scrolled down and there she was, wearing a big smile and holding up a picture of a lobster. The accompanying post said the recipe would appear in her soon-to-be published cookbook. Not the church's cookbook, her cookbook. Hoping to pick up information on some of these FB friends, many of whom were male and had dotted their posts with multiple emojis, I was reading the congratulatory posts when I heard a chair being pushed back in my waiting room. I went to the door, peered out, and saw Greg Lutz sitting staring at the floor, his graying hair wild and uncombed, shoulders slumped, arms hanging down between his legs. I must have made a sound, because he looked up.

"Sorry," he said, "I didn't mean to startle you."

"No, no, it's okay." Walking over to him, I searched for the right words. "Professor Lutz, I can't tell you how terrible I feel about—about Phyllis. To think I was the last person to . . ."

"You weren't the last person."

"Yes, I—oh, you mean whoever . . ."

"I guess you know the police suspect me."

He spoke so softly I had to sit down next to him and lean forward in order to catch his words. "Uh . . . I hadn't heard that, but they always look at the person closest to the victim first. It doesn't mean—"

"I know you were wrongly suspected also and were cleared when they found the real killer. That's why I thought you'd understand and would help me."

I swallowed hard. "I don't know what I can do."

"I remember you had several sessions with my wife a couple of years ago. I wondered if she ever said anything that might help find the person who did this."

"I've just gone through my notes. There's nothing."

"Did she . . . did she ever talk about me—about our relationship?"

I couldn't add to the man's pain. I lied. "Uh . . . I really don't remember. It was a long time ago and she would never let me tape our sessions."

"Did she say why?"

"She had some kind of hang-up. Afraid I was going to hypnotize her, which, of course, I don't do."

He gave a sad, twisted smile. "She was probably afraid you were going to delve into her secret life."

That did startle me. "Did she have one?"

"Secret fantasies. Once she posted on Facebook that she'd been invited to the White House for dinner. Another time it was about being asked to go on *Dancing with the Stars*. She was obsessed with Facebook. She craved attention, and she got lots of it from her Facebook friends. Pretending to have won a cooking contest was just the latest."

"You knew about that?"

"I hadn't. Frazier told me." His eyes filled. "I . . . I still can't believe she's gone. She was several years younger than me, you know. Years ago we . . . she'd had a miscarriage and she was advised not to get pregnant again. It was a huge loss to us both but especially to her—never to be a mother. So I tried to make it up to her. She liked expensive clothes. Recently she wanted cosmetic surgery and a personal trainer, so even though we couldn't afford it I went along. I tried to keep her happy, but lately nothing seemed to . . ."

I had to ask. "Was the reason she went to San Francisco really for a reunion?"

He looked surprised. "That's what she told me. I didn't see any reason to doubt her." Wrinkles suddenly creased his forehead. "I've never met any of her college friends. I can't say for sure who she met there. Did she say anything to you in the airport?"

"She mostly talked about winning the contest." I thought about all those friends on her Facebook page. Had she met someone? Could she have been having an affair? "Would she have gone off with a stranger she met in a bar, do you think?"

"I would have said no, but it appears I didn't know my wife as well as I thought." His voice dropped, became almost inaudible. "I wonder if she was lying to me—if there was someone . . ." He went quiet, trying, I imagined, to wrap his head around the unpleasant possibilities. "She took a cruise to Aruba with a friend a couple of months ago. I couldn't go—work, you know. But I wanted her to enjoy herself." He took a shaky breath. "What if . . . what if she's been seeing someone . . . what if it was a married man and she threatened to tell his wife? Phyllis could do that."

The Phyllis I knew surely could. And she certainly had acted like Greg was no longer in her life. "Uh—maybe there's something on her emails?"

"The police took her computer."

"Oh. Well, they'll be able to access her messages. I looked at her Facebook page and she seemed to have an awful lot of, uh—friends."

"I hadn't thought to do that. I'm not very technical." Slowly he got to his feet. "I guess I should have suspected something. I mean, out of the blue she starts exercising and cooking her own food, diet stuff even though she used to love my cooking. And she dyed her hair blonde . . . why would a woman suddenly do that?"

Why indeed? I felt so sorry for this man. He'd put up with his nasty, sicko wife for all these years, and now he was accused of whacking her when chances are she'd been cheating on him and was going to leave him for some creep who had probably strangled her to shut her up.

"I wish I could help you, Professor. Phyllis and I weren't friends. She never confided in me even when she was a client."

"Yes, I understand that now." He reached down to me and shook my hand so vigorously I thought all the bones would break. "You have helped. Thank you for listening. You've given me food for thought."

At the door, he took his jacket from the coat rack and put it on without bothering to zip it closed. I couldn't help noticing that it seemed too small, his hands sticking out of the sleeves like those of a gangly teenager whose extremities have grown ahead of his body. It gave him an absent-minded professor, lost boy sort of look. My heart ached for him, for what he was probably going to find out about his wife. With a small wave in my direction he left, closing the door behind him.

I sat for some time, feeling depressed and sad thinking about the calamity this foolish, vain, pathological woman had brought on herself and the only man who ever loved her.

Suddenly I wanted to go home, hug my children, and feel my husband's arms around me.

As I got to my feet, my eyes fell on something behind the coat rack that must have fallen out of Lutz's jacket pocket. It looked like a rubber ball, but as I walked over and retrieved it, I realized it was too soft to be a ball. It was a rolled up pair of surgical gloves. Odd. Lutz wasn't a science professor. He was a professor of English Lit . . .

Then, a discordant clanging in my head like crashing cymbals in an out-of-tune orchestra.

Ted's words: "Crime of passion . . . killed her with his bare hands."

My heart started beating fast. Thoughts tumbled. Why had Lutz really come to see me? Why had he asked if Phyllis had told me anything about him, about their relationship? Did he think I knew something that might incriminate him? And the lover, if he existed, was in San Francisco. He couldn't have known Phyllis would be stuck overnight in Philadelphia. At my next thought the gloves fell from my hands, separating as they hit the floor. No fingerprints found. What if Phyllis had called her husband to let him know about missing the connection? What if he'd already been at Newark airport to pick her up when she called and had driven from there to Philadelphia? What if he had used these gloves to—No, he isn't a stupid man. Surely he would have gotten rid of them.

Calm, be calm, I told myself. There could be a million reasons why Lutz had those gloves in his pocket. People use rubber gloves for all sorts of things. This wasn't a life-threatening situation at all. The man clearly had been distraught. He'd teared up when he said he couldn't believe Phyllis was gone. But then . . . a niggling, unrelenting voice in my head— maybe these gloves were in Lutz's pocket in case he needed to silence someone else. Someone he thought might know too much.

I was becoming paranoid. Even if Lutz were guilty, he'd be crazy to call attention to himself by coming after me. The police would make the connection and there'd be no way out for him. I needed to bounce this off Ted. I reached into my pocket for my phone and called him.

"I'm on my way home, honey. What's up?"

Before I could answer, the door opened and Lutz reappeared, an apologetic smile on his face. "I'm very sorry to disturb you again, Ms. Carlin," he said in his quiet voice, "but I seem to have dropped someth—" The smile disappeared as his gaze shifted from the oversize gloves on the floor to the phone I held clutched in my hand.

"Oh dear," he whispered. "I see you've found them."

For one awful moment our eyes met; then he kicked the door shut and flipped the lock.

The click galvanized me. With my free hand I grabbed the heavy wooden coat rack and heaved it in his direction. It caught him off-guard, knocking him to his knees and blocking his path. I make a dash for my office, slammed the door, and shot the bolt.

"Ted, it's Lutz!" I shrieked into the phone. "He's here!"

Over the wild beating of my heart and Ted's shouted questions, I heard what sounded like Lutz dragging the coat rack. Why was he doing that? Could he be planning to use it as a battering ram?

"I've called the police," I yelled, trying and failing to keep the tremor out of my voice. "They'll be here any minute! This is your chance to get away!"

The dragging sound stopped just outside my door. Before I could move or think what else to do, he called out, "I never wanted to hurt you, Ms. Carlin." His voice broke. "I had to do it, you see. The betrayal. After all these years, it was—it was just—the last straw."

If I live to be a hundred I'll never forget the deafening blast of the gunshot, the hideous sound that followed of his body and the coat rack simultaneously crashing to the floor.

LOBSTER FLAMBÉ IN WHISKEY

INGREDIENTS

- 1 small pat of butter
- 1 1½ -2 pound lobster, shelled
- ¼ cup Scotch whiskey
- 1 small can Italian tomatoes without the juice, mashed
- 3-4 tbsp. ketchup
- Drop Pernod or Prunelle
- Dash Worcestershire sauce
- ¼-½ cup good dry sherry
- ½ cup heavy cream
- Salt and pepper to taste
- 1 large sauté pan
- 1 small saucepan
- 1 match

DIRECTIONS

Kill and shell the lobster; if you lack the killer instinct, have some guy at the fish market do it. Melt the butter in the pan. Very briefly sauté the lobster in the butter. Warm the Scotch in a small pot. Pour the warmed Scotch over the lobster and flambé. When the flames have died down, add the tomatoes, ketchup, Pernod, sherry, and Worcestershire sauce. Stir gently. Add the cream and blend into the sauce. Serve immediately. Serves four. Accompany with a crisp white wine, noodles, and salad.

Note: The entire recipe should be completed in ten minutes so that the lobster doesn't toughen.

Dessert

Death at Pinewood Manor

BY MARILYN RAUSCH

MY NAME IS Brandi Severson. I'm the chief homicide detective at the Pine City Police Department. My first name makes me wonder what my mother foresaw as a possible career for me. Exotic dancer perhaps, surely not a law enforcement officer. After watching *Inspector Lewis* on PBS, one of my co-workers dubbed me "Ma'am," like the female homicide chief in the series. Thankfully it stuck.

Our forensics specialist, known as "Prints" by the squad, surveyed the room and blew a soft whistle. "Some joint, isn't it, Ma'am?"

Pinewood Manor's library was covered floor to ceiling with book cases. Two brown leather chairs flanked a fieldstone fireplace, and a mahogany desk the size of a Mini-Cooper sat on a thick Persian rug of deep magenta and sapphire blue hues. Best of all, there was a library ladder that rolled around the shelves. I was itching to climb to the top.

"I feel like we just stepped into an Agatha Christie story. A manor home filled with dinner guests, each with ample opportunity to murder the host. What does the coroner have to say?" I asked.

Prints consulted his notes. "The deceased, Wallace Wellington, excused himself from after-dinner drinks saying he felt unwell, and was found half an hour later in the greenhouse. Seems he was an avid horticulturalist and spent hours there every day. Jeffrey Wyant, our new county coroner, was called after the EMTs determined he was dead. Wyant suspects the victim was poisoned, but that needs to be confirmed by toxicology testing. He said it looks like Mr. Wellington had convulsions and bled out from multiple orifices, signs of poisoning rather than a massive heart event or stroke. The coroner called us with a suspicious death."

Prints smiled and shook his head. "We've got to give the new guy a nickname so he'll feel an official part of our homicide team."

I didn't know Wallace Wellington personally, but he was well-known in Pine City. Worth billions, he was the CEO and major stockholder of Baywater Industries, an international conglomerate. Rumor had it he was a skin-flint and a tyrant. My source of that information was his disgruntled son, whom I dated briefly some years ago . . . but that's another story. Publically, he was respected, his name linked with many charities and do-good causes.

"Make sure no one leaves the premises until I've interviewed everyone. Let's start with whoever prepared the dinner. I assume a place like this has a cook."

Prints checked his notes again. "Yes, Mrs. Grace Potter. She's pretty distraught. I'll show her in and post a patrol outside to insure no one skips out on us."

Grace Potter was the stereotype of a grandmother straight out of Mayberry RFD. Short and plump with Brillo-like gray hair, she looked to be in her 70s. Eyes puffy, she was clutching a shredded tissue. She squinted at me through wire-rimmed glasses. I seated her in one of the leather chairs and sat in the opposite chair.

"This must be very upsetting for you, Mrs. Potter. Have you worked here long?"

She blew her nose and took a deep breath. "I've worked for Mr. Wellington for forty-five years. I live in the carriage house. This family has been very kind to me. I can't imagine what I will do now. What will become of me? Poor Mr. Wellington, such a dear man. He was like a brother to me."

I took a small recorder out of my bag and informed her I would be taping the interview. "Tell me about tonight's meal. Did you prepare all of the food?"

"Oh yes, I prepare all the meals in this house, always from scratch.

Mr. Wellington is . . . oh dear, *was* very particular about his food." She paused and her face paled. "Oh dear, it couldn't have been what he ate. No one else has died or is even sick."

"What was tonight's menu?"

"Spinach-stuffed fish rolls with side dishes of rice pilaf, green beans Almandine, asparagus-artichoke salad, and croissants with honey butter. Triple-layer chocolate cake for dessert. Miss Amanda requested the cake, it's her very favorite. Mr. Anthony picked the wine. I think it was an Italian Pinot Grigio."

"Amanda and Anthony are Mr. Wellington's children, right?" Of course, I knew all too well who Anthony was and didn't cherish the thought of having to question him about his father's unexpected death.

"Yes, I pretty much raised those two, and I suppose I spoil them to this day."

"Did Mr. Wellington eat everything this evening?"

"I really can't say. The dinner was served buffet-style in the main dining room, since it was a large group. I assume he didn't eat the croissants or the cake, of course."

"Why is that?"

"Mr. Wellington adhered to a gluten-free diet and the croissants and cake were made with flour. I baked a little flourless chocolate torte for his dessert."

"Did he eat all of it?"

"No, he left a few bites, not enough to save. I put it in the garbage when I cleaned the table and did the dishes."

"While you were preparing the meal, did anyone else come into the kitchen or have access to the food?"

Mrs. Potter thought for a long time and hesitated. "Just the family members. I was in the kitchen all afternoon, except for a few minutes when I went out to the greenhouse to pick the asparagus."

I scribbled chocolate torte in my notebook and dismissed Mrs. Potter. I placed a quick call to Prints. "Gather the kitchen garbage and send it over to the tox lab with Wyant. Tell him to look for anything chocolate, and then ask Amanda Wellington to join me in the library."

Amanda Wellington was the older of the two Wellington children by about twelve years. She was in her mid-forties, but looked much younger. My first thought, although unkind, was that she had some work done on her too-flawless face. Blonde, slender, and dressed in a form-fitting, sleeveless sheath of hot pink, she screamed *Barbie Doll*. Unlike Mrs. Potter, she looked far from distressed at the death of her father.

She sat in one of the leather chairs, crossed her bare tan legs, and glared at me with a stony face. I ignored her demeanor and proceeded with my questioning. "Amanda, are you currently living here at Pinewood?"

"Yes, I moved back here temporarily after my divorce last year. My new villa in Barcelona is under construction. I hope to be out of here as soon as possible," she said, fingering what looked like a religious medal on a gold chain around her neck.

"How would you describe your relationship with your father?"

She snorted a dry, humorless laugh. "I think the word would be 'tempestuous.' Oh, I admired him and respected him, but I also detested him. He was a controlling, abusive bastard at times, but I loved him. My analyst has a heyday with my wildly-conflicting daddy issues."

Wow. I could say this much for her, the girl didn't hold back. "Do you know of anyone who might want him out of the way? Anyone who might have a grudge against him?"

She smiled for the first time in our interview. "Do you have all day, detective? The list would reach from here to Hades. No one runs a successful international enterprise without making enemies. Many of tonight's guests are business associates who have been screwed by my father in one way or another over the years."

"Thank you. That's all for now. We'll talk again later and get your official statement about the events of this evening. Would you please ask your brother to come to the library now?"

As I walked with her to the door, I stopped her a moment. "I was admiring your lovely necklace. Is it a saint's medal?"

She pressed her hand over the medal. "Yes, Saint Valentine, the patron saint of lovers."

I dreaded seeing Anthony Wellington again. We'd had a short but passionate romance over ten years ago. It was never to be. I was from the other side of the tracks, not cultured enough for a trust fund Ivy League college student. Apparently, I was his summer fling who got flung at the end of the season. I hadn't talked with him since, although I continued to follow him in the society pages. I sat up straight, telling myself to be cool and professional. Then he sauntered into the room.

My composure went right down the biffy with a double flush, as I embarrassingly began to swoon over him like a friggin' tweener. "Hi, Tony, you're looking as handsome as ever." *Jeez, what kind of tough homicide detective starts an interview with that line?*

Tony smiled, revealing his orthodontically-perfect teeth and the deep dimples in his sculptured face. He was wearing jeans, a crisp white shirt with the tails out, and a finely-tailored blazer. No socks with his tasseled loafers. "I heard you were a police detective, Brandi. Quite a surprise, I must say. It's good seeing you again."

I focused on my notepad as I started the interview, hoping he didn't sense my unease. I cleared my throat. "I'm so sorry for your loss. You must be in shock. I just have a few questions, things I need to clarify for the investigation of your father's death. Was this evening's dinner a routine event or a special occasion?"

He sat, leisurely put one leg over his opposite knee, and templed his hands. "Father always had an agenda, but he became ill before revealing it," he replied. "I suspect he was going to announce that he was stepping down and naming me CEO of Baywater Industries."

"So what happens now?"

He shrugged his shoulders. "It's up to the Board of Directors, and a couple of those old codgers hanging out in the parlor think I am too young to take over. I may be out of a job."

"Do you have any idea of who might have wanted to do harm to your father?"

To my shock, he answered quickly. "As a matter of fact, I do. Last week I stopped by to see Mrs. Potter. As you know, Mother died when I was ten, and Mrs. Potter is more a mother to me than my own mother ever was. I overheard an argument out in the greenhouse between Father and Javier. It was pretty heated, and since Javier is now gone, I assume father fired him."

"Who is Javier?"

Tony smirked. "Now that's the million dollar question. Supposedly Javier Silva is a Brazilian expert on tropical plants. My father hired him to cultivate rare species in his greenhouse."

I cocked my head. "Supposedly . . . ?"

"I suspect he is more likely a gardener. A charming con man, if you want my opinion. Once when I called him Cabana Boy, Mrs. Potter scolded me. She was rather taken with him, but I didn't trust the guy."

"Thanks for your time, Tony. Our forensics team will be here for several more hours, but I won't have any more questions until later. It was good seeing you again."

He stood and touched my arm. "Maybe when this is all over, Brandi, we could have dinner. For old time's sake."

I could feel the heat rise in my face and neck. I smiled weakly and mumbled, "Sure. That would be nice."

For the next three hours I interviewed all the guests—members of the Baywater Board of Directors and a few of their wives, including one young tootsie who was obviously a trophy for one of the oldest members. None was willing to say ill of the dead or air any dirty laundry. It was as if they had already colluded and devised the official corporate statement about their former leader . . . a wonderful man whom they admired and will sorely miss. There was a hint a new CEO was going to be named, and that it might be someone from outside the company.

The first few days of a homicide investigation are intense. There is a lot of data to gather, many leads to follow, a shitload of paperwork, press conferences, interviews with reporters, tip calls (both valuable and bogus), and family and friends and interest groups clamoring for justice. Just as it is with a missing person's case, the first 48 hours are crucial. I don't sleep. I survive on espresso, candy, and adrenaline.

At three a.m. I departed Pinewood Manor and returned to my townhouse. I headed for the office in my spare bedroom. I suppose I could call it my library. It does have a ratty green recliner salvaged from my parents' basement and a bookcase from Ikea. My mind jumped from a possible dinner with Tony to flourless chocolate tortes to the mysterious missing Javier. I wandered to the kitchen, plugged in the espresso machine, and tore open a jumbo package of fun-sized Snickers.

I took my caffeine-loaded dinner back to my office, opened my laptop, and logged into the department site, where I found Wyant's preliminary report: probable cause of death by poisoning. I sent an email to Sergeant Walkowski (aka "Ski") to check criminal and immigration records for Javier Silva. I surfed the web for information about Baywater Industries to learn more about the company and to try to determine who might have a motive to bump off its leader.

Then I ventured off the grid and googled Anthony Wellington. The first link was a photo of him at a charity benefit for CaringBridge. His arm was around a very pretty woman who reminded me of the actress Anne Hathaway. I went no further and mentally erased dinner with Tony off my date book, which was otherwise completely blank.

For the heck of it, I looked to see if there was a patron saint for police officers, and Saint Michael popped up. I searched Amazon for a Saint Michael necklace and saw Amanda's Saint Valentine medal . . . Saint Valentine, patron saint of lovers and of small intimate gardens.

I showered, dressed, and headed for the station at five a.m. By noon I had confirmation: Wellington was poisoned with strychnine in his chocolate torte. It's a fast-acting poison, and it fit with the timetable of events and the victim's condition.

It didn't take long for Ski to locate Silva and establish his alibi for the murder. He was being held in a deportation center in El Paso, Texas. The El Paso PD would be bringing him in for questioning. Cabana Boy had a criminal record on both sides of the border, mainly larceny and fraud, including a long history of bilking rich women.

Ski, Prints, and I sat down at the end of the day to review the case. We compiled a list of questions. I wrote them on our white board.

Who had an opportunity to slip poison in the chocolate torte?

Why was Javier Silva dismissed? Does it have anything to do with Wellington's murder?

Who would gain by his death? Who would lose?

"It's pretty obvious, isn't it, men?" I said. "Wallace Wellington must have found out about Javier Silva's criminal history or illegal immigration status. Or, he possibly caught on to the fact his daughter was having an affair with Silva. For whatever reason, he dismissed him, infuriating Amanda."

I gleefully paced around the squad room, spinning out the rest of the solution to Wellington's murder. "Amanda Wellington requested a cake for dessert that she knew her father couldn't eat, thus the preparation of his own special dessert. She laced the chocolate torte with strychnine when Mrs. Potter went to pick asparagus."

"Silva's past history must be leading you to conclude Amanda and Silva were having an affair, right?" asked Prints.

"That and a couple other clues, too. Amanda mentioned she was building a villa in Spain. I bet she was planning to elope with Silva. Her necklace with the patron saint of lovers and intimate gardens was another clue. I saw it online for $29.99. There's no way she would wear cheap jewelry unless it was a gift from a lover."

I pulled my cell phone out of my pocket and checked the time. Less than 48 hours, and I was sure I had solved the murder of Wallace Wellington. "Ski, bring Amanda Wellington in for questioning, and be sure to read her Miranda Rights to her."

MRS. POTTER'S FLOURLESS CHOCOLATE TORTE

INGREDIENTS

- 1½ sticks (12 tbsp.) unsalted butter, cut into small pieces
- 12 oz. bittersweet chocolate, chopped
- 6 large eggs
- ½ cup sugar
- Pinch of sea salt
- Powdered sugar for dusting

DIRECTIONS

Preheat the oven to 350 degrees. Lightly butter the bottom and side of a 9-inch springform pan. Combine the chocolate and 1½ sticks butter in a heatproof bowl. Place the bowl over a saucepan of simmering water (do not let the bowl touch the water) and stir until melted and combined. Remove the bowl from the saucepan and let cool slightly. Combine the eggs, sugar and salt in a large bowl. Beat with a mixer on medium-high speed until pale and thick, 5-8 minutes.

Gently fold half of the melted chocolate mixture into the egg mixture until just combined, and then gently fold in the rest. Pour the batter into the prepared pan. Bake until the top is no longer shiny and barely jiggles and a toothpick inserted into the center comes out with only a few crumbs (35-45 minutes). Transfer to a rack and let cool completely in the pan. Remove the springform ring and transfer to a platter; dust with powdered sugar.

Eat, Pray, and Maybe Die

BY COLIN NELSON

POISON. IF HE was going to do it, poison might work best. Ethylene glycol was colorless, odorless, and slightly sweet to the taste. It would be fatal in under an hour and difficult to detect. A food chemist at GMO Food Company, Bob Crane daydreamed about the mechanisms to deliver the poison. *A fancy cocktail. Perfect. But an autopsy could be risky.*

His boss, Lois Conrad, had fired Bob's lover from her job in the lab where they both worked. "Doesn't fit our culture," Conrad had said. Crushed, Terri had left town—and Bob. He would never forgive Conrad for ruining his only chance at happiness.

Maybe Bob could use a gun to the head. Easy, quick, fatal. But then he'd have to find an unregistered gun and learn to use it. And with all the technology available to crime scene detectives, he was sure they could trace a gun to him somehow.

Drowning? Car accident? He realized it was actually difficult to kill someone you hated and get away with it. He could go to her house and whack her in the head with a brick or heavy pan. *Too messy. Too much evidence could be left behind.*

Standing in his own kitchen, Bob waited for the "boss from hell." In a few minutes some of his friends from work would also arrive. He'd scheduled the brunch prior to Conrad's firing of Terri. Reluctantly, he had decided to keep the date—if for nothing else to try and stay on Conrad's good side himself.

Contentiously divorced, he was paying exorbitant child support payments for his daughter, Ava. Bob didn't begrudge the higher costs, but now his salary was stretched to the breaking point. He had been lonely for years, until he met Terri. Her memory hung on like a ghost.

He unscrewed a bottle of dried cilantro and sniffed. Not good enough, he decided. This meal must be special for his friends. Bob pulled out a bunch of cilantro from the refrigerator. It smelled grassy and sweet and left a spicy prickle in his nose.

Mexican food was everyone's favorite. Bob had chosen that for the main course: Bobby Flay's ranch-style eggs with chorizo and tomato-red chili sauce.

He set his bamboo cutting board on the counter and placed eight ounces of chorizo sausages on it. The recipe said to remove the skins, so Bob went to the drawer next to the sink. His fingers crawled over the handles of the Wusthof knives.

He cupped a sausage in his palm. It felt as soft as a baby's skin. He inserted the tip of the steel knife at the lower end of the meat and pricked the skin, sliding the blade underneath. *What would it feel like to plunge the knife into living flesh?* Bob worked upward along the length of the sausage. When he got to the top end, he used his fingers to spread the skin and unwrap it carefully from the meat inside. He inhaled the aroma, spicy with hints of hot, dry deserts far to the south of his home in Minneapolis.

Conrad had been his boss for three years—three years of hell. In her fifties, she had put on weight but still wore short skirts that were as tight as the skins he'd just stripped off the sausages. The arrogant, ignorant "drill sergeant" oversaw Bob's research lab.

With her as his boss, Bob's workload had doubled. That made her team meetings even more maddening. The Bitch, as the women called her, scheduled them, and everyone was expected to attend. Bob flashed back to the meeting last week. She had made her entrance twelve minutes late while seven people waited. When Conrad sat down, her phone hummed the Neil Diamond song "Cracklin' Rosie." It sounded like a social call. After eight minutes of moronic chatter, she hung up and dismissed everyone. Bob had lost over an hour from his pending projects, and he knew there would be hell to pay.

He searched through his wine and selected a Montepulciano for the chili sauce. Bob removed a sauce pan from the lower cupboard. He set it on the stove and added canola oil to heat up. He arranged the sausage into the pan. With a wooden spoon Bob crumbled the meat. It sizzled and released a pungent aroma of spices.

The doorbell rang. With long strides, Bob loped through the living room to the front door. He opened it to see Jo Ann, the chemist who worked in the lab next to his. She smiled, stood on her tiptoes, and pecked him on the cheek. "Hey, it's Emeril himself." She laughed.

"Naw, you're too skinny." Her hair smelled like herbal shampoo.

Bob hurried back to the kitchen, followed by Jo Ann. "Thanks for coming early. I could use some help."

Jo Ann clinked a bottle of Jose Cuervo Blanco tequila onto the counter. Next to that she emptied a mesh bag of limes. They rolled around in crooked paths. "This okay for your margaritas?"

"Sure. I make 'em from scratch." Bob hovered over the spitting sauce pan. He used a slotted wooden spoon to lift out the golden brown meat and set the clumps onto some paper towels. "I'll be sure to give Conrad a triple shot. That'll finish her off."

"You should substitute drain cleaner," Jo Ann whispered.

"Too messy. I'd have to clean up."

"Okay, I know I promised not to talk about her, but you know what she pulled yesterday?"

Bob snapped a can opener onto a can of Hunt's Whole Peeled Plum Tomatoes and twisted the handle as it crawled around the rim. "Nothing will surprise me."

"Okay, so she's always saying her nephew's got ADHD, right? Well, she ordered me to head-up a charitable drive for an ADHD counseling center. Not even remotely work related! Wasting company resources! Ask me, I think the kid needs to get out of her clutches."

"He's a charity that's always been close to your heart." Bob kidded Jo Ann.

"Shut up. Okay, I know damn well once I've worked my ass off, Conrad will take the credit."

"She always does."

Jo Ann pounded her fist on the counter. "Take that, you freak!" she shouted. "Not that I'm defending her, but I'm impressed that she has taken such good care of her nephew. Too bad Conrad can't bring some of that charity into the office."

Bob looked at the counter next to Jo Ann. "Meanwhile, squeeze the limes for the margaritas. I'll prepare one for the she-wolf of the SS." He emptied the tomatoes into a small bowl and poured almost all the oil out of the pan. Next, he rolled a Spanish yellow onion onto the cutting board. He selected the chef's knife, twelve inches long and almost two inches deep.

Gripping it tightly, he cut down in the middle of the onion. The skin crackled, clear juice ran out, and the left side fell away. Bob blinked as the oils floated up into his eyes. Placing the tip of the knife on the board, he levered the blade up and down across the rings to chop them. He heard the crisp sound of the blade severing the pieces into square chunks. While his eyes stung, the sound of the knife chunked against the bamboo over and over.

Bob thought of Terri. It had been such a struggle for Bob to date again after the debilitating divorce, but Terri had coaxed him along. Bob's vacant and narrow life had blossomed for the first time. Now without Terri, his future collapsed like a dead plant before winter.

"I got a better story," Bob said to Jo Ann. "Last summer Conrad got tickets for a Twin's baseball game. Said it would be a 'team building' event. But there was no requirement to attend, so I spent the day with Ava. Did I get shit from her! Told me it would definitely affect my future with the company." He poured tequila, lime juice, and triple sec into a steel shaker filled with ice. Bob shook it roughly and heard the ice clatter against the steel. He poured out two drinks into frosted glasses.

"That's bullshit." Jo Ann sipped her drink. "Oh, is this good."

"Glad you like it. Cooking and entertaining are about the only things that give me pleasure anymore."

Jo Ann's face wrinkled. "I bet Conrad will be late, as usual, so she can make a grand entrance."

"When she drives, the sun visor is always down so she can look in the mirror all the time." Bob used the knife to scrape the chopped onions into the pan. "All she talks about are her problems. Her job, her weight, her heart problems. It's only her malicious personality that keeps her going."

Bob unwrapped five cloves of garlic. Using the flat side of the chef's knife, he placed it on top of a clove and smacked the blade with his palm. Smashing a skull would feel good. Underneath, the garlic split open and the husk fell off, leaving the smashed cloves. He tossed the garlic in the pan with the onions and watched it turn walnut brown as it released a pungent odor.

He glanced at the watch that hung loose on his wrist. "Dammit! I forgot to fix a dessert." He sighed. "I want this to be perfect, so that you can't even detect my presence in the preparation."

Jo Ann said, "Don't worry. You've got all this fruit for dessert. Who else is coming?"

"Gary and Maureen."

"Gary?" Jo Ann's eyes opened wide. She slammed the margarita glass on the counter. "Are you really being mean? Do you know what our beloved leader did to him?"

"No, what?" He turned down the heat on the pan.

"She gave him a big research project. Told him he was completely in charge. Okay, she interfered every half hour for days until he finally snapped. I know this is a time when you guys are supposed to let your feminine side out, but for God's sake, the guy actually cried."

"That's horrible." On the cutting board, Bob lined up a bright red jalapeno pepper, an ancho chili, and a pasilla chili that was black and shriveled like a raisin on steroids. They looked harmless lying there. But the combined heat of these ingredients could be deadly hot. Bob stretched on a pair of latex gloves and used his paring knife to attack the jalapeno pepper first.

Maybe he should add a ghost chili to sear the lungs, throat, and tongue. Wouldn't kill her, but would cause great pain. Bob smiled.

The sharp blade hesitated at the resistance of the outer skin. Bob sawed back and forth and burst through into the soft flesh underneath. The pungent smell irritated his nose. He chopped the pepper over and over. The recipe called for a coarse cut, but he got carried away and mutilated the pieces until they were scattered over the board in tiny bits.

The front door bell rang again.

Bob took a deep breath, stopped cutting, and went to open the door. Maureen reached up to give him a loose hug. Their faces didn't touch. "Sorry I'm early," she said.

"No problem. JoAnn's here, and I'm making margaritas." Bob stepped aside as she walked toward the kitchen. Maureen opened her offering: two bags of tortillas. "I could only find flour, no corn. Sorry it's not more authentic."

Bob stripped off the gloves and waved his hand to indicate that was all right. "I still have to make the chili sauce." He pulled out another sauce pan and set it on the stove.

"Why are you being so nice to the Wicked Witch of the West?" Maureen asked him.

JoAnn said, "He's sucking up for a promotion."

"Hope you have better luck than me. She told me that with my resume I wasn't promotable," Maureen said. "Don't tell anyone, but I'm out of the lab as soon as I can find anything else." She accepted a drink from Bob.

He nodded with understanding. "I'm really doing this for all of you. And considering how she dumped Terri, it doesn't hurt for me to stay on her good side."

Maureen shrugged. "I hope you're right."

Bob glanced away to avoid answering. Terri's ghost always hovered near Bob. "Hey, someone's at the door."

She left the kitchen and came back with Gary. He was short with red hair and a bushy beard. From a paper bag he lifted out a six-pack of

Corona beer, slick with moisture. "Hey, man. Put these in the fridge." He high-fived Bob. "Dude, the only reason I'm here is you. I sure as hell wouldn't come for her."

"We could write a new TV series, *Horrible Bosses*." Jo Ann laughed.

From the top cupboard, Bob lowered a Cuisinart food processor onto the counter. He poured the plum tomatoes into the top of the processor and watched as the red globs splashed over the gleaming blades at the bottom. Dump her in a cement mixer.

Bob added one cup of the wine to the pan with the onions and chorizo. As the mixture thickened, he scraped the coating off the bottom of the pan. He felt the glaze breaking up and increased the pressure. The glaze cracked and broke into jagged pieces that Bob smashed with the flat end of the wooden spoon.

Maureen stirred her margarita with a fingertip. The citrus smell wafted through the kitchen. "Uh, anyone know about the rumors of some more lay-offs?"

"Huh?" Bob felt a jolt shoot through his chest. The payments for his daughter were already bankrupting him. He couldn't afford to lose his job.

Gary took a long drink of Corona. "Dude, haven't you heard?"

"What?" Bob stopped working over the pan. He could tell by the tone of Gary's voice that something was wrong.

Gary wiped his mouth with the back of his hand. "Dude, the Bitch is clearing out the labs."

"What's that mean?" Bob felt his chest tighten.

"Just a rumor, but I know someone who knows the vice president." Gary moved next to Bob and curved an arm over his shoulders. "All I know is, your lab's in the line of fire. I hope you don't get shot, dude."

"But—" The memory of Terri's departure at Conrad's hands settled on Bob. He struggled to catch his breath.

Jo Ann must have seen how devastated he was; she slid over to put her arm around his waist. "You could call off the brunch. We'd understand."

Bob mumbled, "No, no, that's okay. You guys are here and everything's almost ready."

He circled the kitchen for a few minutes. His head popped up. "I've got some time now to make some banana bread for dessert."

He found the large mixing bowl and sloshed in all the ingredients. Dipping an electric mixer into the bowl, he beat the yolk of the eggs to splatter against the side. Increasing the speed of the mixer, he pummeled the ingredients. Shaking a handful of walnuts into the Cuisinart, he watched as the blades pulverized them. He ladled the contents into a baking pan and smacked the mixture with a spoon so hard it almost slopped over the sides as he shoved it into the oven.

What about a tanning bed "accident?"

They all moved into the living room and kept drinking to get prepared for their nemesis.

An hour later, Conrad finally arrived. She paused at the door, waited until everyone had looked toward her, and walked in. Without looking at Bob, she shoved past him. From the center of the room, she announced, "I'm thirsty." Her breath smelled stale.

Bob fought to control himself as he thought about how much he wanted to kill her right on the spot. About how he could use the frying pan to bash her head senseless and how the chorizo and oil would fly all over, mixed with blood and bits of her brain. He stopped and took a deep breath.

Alone in the kitchen, Bob mixed a special margarita for Conrad. After pouring it into a stemmed glass, he washed out the shaker thoroughly.

She grabbed it without thanks and slurped the opaque lime liquid. She ordered a second one from Bob and they all waited, hungry, for almost an hour while she finished her drinks.

Then Bob cracked eggs into a frying pan; added the chorizo, salt, and pepper; and turned the heat too high, almost burning the mixture. He set two eggs, crisp and brown around the edges, on top of a warm tortilla on each plate, and Jo Ann served them.

"Put the tomato chili sauce on top," Bob told them and turned to Conrad. Staring at her, he said, "Hope it's not too hot for you." He didn't smile.

She grunted. "I love it hot, but my cardiologist told me to watch it. Seems I've got some new issues." She waited for anyone to console her. No one spoke.

During brunch, the conversation teetered from one topic to another, everyone careful not to mention work. For dessert, Bob returned from the kitchen with a brown loaf of banana bread.

He set it directly in front of Conrad. "For you. A special recipe my grandma always made."

"I don't like dessert," Conrad said. She pushed the bread away. When she saw his expression, she growled, "Oh, for God's sake. You're always begging for something. Okay."

Holding a serrated bread knife to sever a slice from the loaf, Bob approached her from behind her neck. He glanced down and moved to the bread. He sawed off a slice and handed it to his boss.

She propped both elbows on the table and ate quickly. "It's okay, Bobby." Her breath wheezed, and she leaned forward to cough.

Bob watched her.

Conrad leaned back again, and Bob could see her throat working as if she couldn't swallow. "Are you okay?" Bob asked.

"Don't know." Conrad panted and rocked back and forth. A red flush rose from her chest to grab her neck. She stopped moving and sat straight up. She took a long drink of mineral water and said, "Better. Hope it's not the old heart." Conrad flashed a weak smile. No one said anything. "I think I'm okay."

Bob stared at her.

In a few minutes, the flush spread across her face. She tilted to the side. "Dizzy—"

Maureen jumped up, her chair clattering onto the floor behind her. "Shouldn't we call 911? Someone?"

"Yeah," Gary agreed.

Maureen ran around the end of the table to stand beside Conrad, but didn't touch her.

"My chest . . . can't breathe . . ." her words slurred. "Aargh!" she screamed. Sweat spread across her face. It smelled metallic.

Maureen hopped from one foot to the other. "That does it. I'm calling." She ran into the bedroom where she'd left her purse.

Bob remained on his side of the table. He watched as Conrad fell off the chair and her body thudded onto the floor. Her legs quivered and her arms jerked to the sides. Then, she rolled over onto her back and stared with red, unconscious eyes toward the ceiling.

A half hour later, after the emergency medics had done all they could for her, they told the stunned group she was dead.

"Heart attack?" Gary asked.

The older man shrugged. "Can't say. Could be. Does she have family?"

"She told us she had some heart issues," Jo Ann interrupted.

The group looked up from the body on the floor to Bob. He picked up three plates and Conrad's cocktail glass and washed them off thoroughly in the kitchen. When he returned, their eyes silently questioned him. He frowned and said, "Maybe it really was too hot."

"The family won't want an autopsy," the older man said. He heaved himself up and wobbled on his front leg for an instant before he nodded to his assistant to bag the body.

BANANA CHOCOLATE CURRY PECAN BREAD

INGREDIENTS

- 1 cup butter
- 2 cups white sugar
- 2 eggs
- 2 tbsp. mayonnaise
- 6 mashed bananas
- 3 cups all-purpose flour
- 1½ tsp. curry
- 1 tsp. cinnamon
- ½ tsp. ground ginger
- ½ tsp. salt
- 1 tsp. baking powder
- 2 tsp. baking soda
- 1 cup semi-sweet chocolate chips
- ½ cup chopped pecans

DIRECTIONS

Preheat oven to 350 degrees. Lightly grease two 9 x 5 loaf pans. In a large bowl, cream together the shortening and sugar until light and fluffy. Stir in the eggs one at a time, beating well with each addition. Stir in the mayonnaise and bananas. Stir together the flour, salt, curry, cinnamon, ground ginger, baking powder, and baking soda. Blend the flour mixture into the banana mixture; stir just enough to evenly combine. Fold in the chocolate chips and pecans. Bake at 350 degrees for 60-75 minutes or until a toothpick inserted into the center of the loaf comes out clean. You should be able to see the loaf pull away from the pan at this point. Cool loaf in the pan for 20 minutes.

Whole Lotta Bull

BY SUSAN KOEFOD

MENDOTA COUNTY DETECTIVE Arvo Thorson finished his second Pronto Pup shortly before he arrived at the murder scene. He elbowed his way through the crowd gathered outside the Creative Activities building, his notebook in hand and a suitably grim look on his face.

He hoped no one would notice that his shirt was stained with the telltale sign of French's yellow mustard.

The Minnesota State Fair was in full swing. Already at nine a.m. on a hot, late August Tuesday, thousands of potential suspects could have come and gone through the clacking turnstiles. The perpetrator could easily be miles away by now. Any delay, even for a mouthwatering Pronto Pup or two, would be inexcusable.

Except that in this case, the apparent murderer had already been shot dead by the Falcon Heights police. The press had already opened and shut this sensational case in the space of three hours, as was neatly summarized by a morning DJ.

"Rampaging Bull Gores Pie Contest Judge! That's right, you heard it here first on F-A-I-R RADIO!"

The press had gotten ahead of the facts, as usual, thought Thorson. And at the moment, there were only three facts, all of which Detective Thorson duly noted in his dime-store notebook:

1. Betty Bruckle, the State Fair pie judge, was dead, a gaping stab wound in her chest. Her body was slumped next to the prize jam and jelly case.

2. A 1,500-pound Black Angus bull had been shot dead by the local police department. It lay in a heap twenty feet away from the dead judge, a display of lacey doilies and antimacassars nearby.

3.   The blue-ribbon strawberry rhubarb pie baked by Barbie Bruckle, the judge's sister-in-law, was missing.

A teary young boy wearing an FFA shirt sat next to the bull's carcass, his arm around the black beast's neck, his hand softly caressing the massive forehead.

"This your bull, young man?" Thorson asked softly.

The slight, freckled boy, who couldn't be more than twelve or thirteen, nodded. It seemed impossible that the huge bull belonged to this fragile young lad. Yet the animal had obviously been much fussed over—its black coat was shiny as obsidian and smoothed clean of loose hairs, and its hooves were manicured far better than Thorson's stubby, chewed nails would ever be.

The boy protectively cradled the dead bull's head in his lap, his fingers absently massaging the bull's velvety ears.

"I . . . don't understand. Cuddles . . . wouldn't hurt nobody." The boy dragged his forearm under his snotty nose.

"Cuddles. . . . That's the bull's name?"

"Yes sir, it is."

"What's your name, son?" Thorson asked.

"Lyle. Johnson."

The boy announced his name with the force of a slap; clearly he was growing angrier by the moment. "I raised Cuddles from a runt calf. I know him like he was my own flesh and blood. He wouldn't hurt nobody, no sir."

"Do you have any idea how he got here, all the way across the fairgrounds?"

"No. I got to his pen at six a.m. and the door was wide open. I ran down every street, calling for him. When I heard the gunshots in the distance, I couldn't believe what I was hearing."

The boy glanced at the dead bull and then looked back at Thorson with a resolute and certain expression in his baby blues. By Thorson's estimation, the boy had suddenly matured a good four or five years in the space of thirty seconds.

"He didn't kill that lady, no sir. He's been framed, isn't that what they call it? I'm an honest kid and I know Cuddles through and through. He didn't murder anyone."

Thorson realized something was missing from the bull. He leaned in and whispered something in the boy's ears.

"No sir. They never do," the boy answered.

Thorson patted the boy on the shoulder and thanked him.

One of the Falcon Heights cops motioned to Thorson.

"Bill, isn't it?" Thorson asked with his hand out.

"That's right, you've got a good memory. We haven't seen you out here for ten years, is it? That was the year the Department had a booth in the Grandstand. You were here with your beautiful wife and little girl. I remember how your missus laughed when she tried the breathalyzer. How are those two lovely ladies?"

Thorson flinched and hoped Bill hadn't noticed. The divorce had only become final in the past few months. Helen had wanted out for pretty much all of those ten years; when he finally gave in, she quickly moved on, even asking him to babysit the very next weekend when she went on her first post-divorce date. With the same man she'd been seeing on the side for a decade. Apparently the gossip hadn't made its way to Falcon Heights yet.

He was still in love with her. No one knew why, least of all Thorson.

"They're fine," he said quickly. "You know something about this witness?"

"Yeah, some carney by the name of MacGregor."

Thorson flipped open his notebook and jotted down the name.

"What's his story?"

"He's new at the Fair this year. Mechanic at the fun house. He's from down south, Louisiana or Oklahoma."

"Aren't they all . . ."

"You bet."

Thorson underlined Louisiana and Oklahoma. His stomach growled. He wondered whether there was a Tom Thumb mini-donuts stand nearby.

"Only thing we have is this carney saying he stepped into a stinking fresh pile of bull manure sometime past 5:30 a.m. as he was walking into St. Urho's Dining Hall. They have him over there now waiting for you, though I don't know why. It's pretty clear the bull wandered over here, passed St. Urho's, got in here and gored that poor lady."

"I'm not so sure the bull did it. I mean, look at the size of him. I would have expected to see more blood-stained hoof prints, more signs of a struggle, more damage to all of these display cases. I mean, that's a lot of bull, Bill, and this place is practically a china shop. And you seemed to have missed a pretty significant bit of evidence here."

"What's that, Detective?"

Thorson looked at the tear-stained boy again. "That bull hasn't got any horns. That's why they call Angus 'polled.' They never have any horns."

"Oh," the cop said, embarrassed.

Thorson kneeled next to Lyle again and put a hand on the boy's shoulder. "I'm sorry, son. I've got some work to do now." He handed the boy his card. "If you notice or hear anything else, I want you to call me."

Thorson headed out to see MacGregor at the Dining Hall. The weather was fine, sunny, and still. The thick, heavy air smelled of all manner of dipped and fried things: cheese curds, onion blossoms, candy bars, and chocolate wrapped bacon. Under the sweet and oily smells, there was another pungent one. Body odor. It was going to be a hot one.

Thorson walked down Cosgrove and sure enough, there was a mini-donut booth right at the Dan Patch intersection. He traded a couple of dollars for a hot, greasy, sugary bag of mini-donuts, consuming them in a flash and licking his fingers clean. He'd get some coffee at St. Urho's. His cell phone buzzed. It was Helen, texting him: "U R late again!"

He cursed when he remembered. The alimony check. He texted back. "Sorry. Tonight."

He arrived in front of St. Urho's Dining Hall and ritualistically touched the chain-saw sculpture of the legendary Finn, said to have cast frogs out of Finland by his loud voice. Legend had it that Urho loved sour milk and fish soup, both of which were prominently featured on the Dining Hall's menu though they were seldom ordered. Thorson's mother had been Finnish, his father Swedish, a mixed marriage according to Minnesota Scandinavian immigrant standards. Despite that handicap, their marriage had lasted a lifetime, fifty years. Thorson's had sputtered out after the first year, though they'd doggedly carried on with the hollow sham for ten.

The carney was sitting in a dark booth in the back, hunched over a plate of pie. When Thorson sat down across from him, the man cowered. He seemed nervous. Too nervous.

A waitress walked over with Thorson's cup of coffee.

"You want some coffee?" Thorson asked the carney.

He nodded and smiled slightly, revealing a mouth full of broken and missing teeth. Thorson was starting to prefer the cowering version. He didn't want to see those teeth.

The basic information had already been taken down by the local police, one of whom was standing nearby. Thorson scanned through the carney's demographics. Ferdinand MacGregor. Birthplace: Baton Rouge. Age: 46 or 47, he's not sure. Permanent address: none.

"You go by Ferdinand?"

"People call me Nando."

"Um. Okay, Nando. So why don't you tell me what happened this morning."

Nando casually speared a forkful of pie from what remained on his plate as he relayed a story that was not too different from what Bill had already told him.

"You said you came here around five a.m.?"

"Around then. It was early."

"Sun up yet?"

"Yeah. Sure. The sun was up." Nando dragged his finger across his plate, dabbing up the bright red sticky juice.

"Seems to me that it might have been later than five a.m. When I drove into work this morning at 6:30, it was still dark. Are you sure the sun was up when you got here?"

"When I got here," Nando sucked on his finger. "Now, you may be right about that, sir. Maybe it was later. Yes. You're right. I think it was more like 7:30."

"So it was 7:30. You got here at St. Urho's. You're walking up to the front door. Then what happens."

"I stepped right into that bulls—I mean dung. I stepped into it."

"Tell me more about that. Do you remember whether it seemed like it was fresh or not? Had it been there awhile?"

"Well, it sure seemed pretty fresh to me. I don't know much about cows. Alligators, that's more what I know." He threw his head back and laughed; Thorson looked away to avoid the sight of the teeth.

"Do you remember whether it seemed hot? Or cold? Solid or not much?"

"I can't really remember all of that. I know I had to clean off my boots before I came in here."

Nando picked up his plate and gave it a final lick.

"That must have been some pie," Thorson said. "What was it? Strawberry rhubarb?"

"Yes it was."

"I think I might order some myself." Thorson had already made note of St. Urho's menu. No pie of any kind. Ever. He'd been coming to St. Urho's for years and had never seen pie on the menu.

The cowering expression returned. "I think they're out for today."

Thorson called the cop over.

"Mr. Nando, would you mind showing me what you have in that bag on your lap?"

"Umm." Nando was trying to think fast, Thorson could see it in his eyes. "Well, sure. Why not?" He handed the bag to Thorson.

Thorson opened it and saw a half-eaten pie. He lifted the pie pan slowly out of the bag. The filling was a fire-red mixture of fibrous rhubarb and chunky strawberries. A blue ribbon dangled beneath it.

"Hmm. No wonder it's good. It won the blue ribbon. Seems to have been baked by a B. Bruckle."

"I don't know anything about that, officer. Some guy gave it to me this morning. He just ran by and handed it to me. I don't know anything else but that."

Something else was stuck to the bottom of the pie pan. It was a ticket stub with writing on it, stained red with strawberry-rhubarb sauce.

"I think you'll need to head down to the station for more questioning, Mr. MacGregor. A lot more questioning. At the moment, you're looking more like an accessory to a murder, possibly the prime suspect, unless you have a better explanation for how you and this pie came together this morning."

That was enough for the cork to come out of Nando. A skinny middle-aged man had stopped him late the previous night with a strange request and a $100 bill. First thing in the morning, Nando was to bring some fresh manure from the cattle pens over to St. Urho's and dump it out front. If anyone asked, he was to tell the story of having come upon it in the wee hours of the morning and stepped into it when it was fresh. The man had dropped by St. Urho's this morning and nodded at Nando, handing him the bag with the pie and another $100 for his troubles. Nando knew enough to not ask many questions about this kind of assignment.

"You need to be available for more questioning. Don't even consider leaving the fairgrounds until we've said you can, do you understand?"

"Yes sir."

Nando got up to leave. "I suppose I can't have the rest of that pie."

"You are correct."

Thorson's phone buzzed again. It was another text from his ex. "Where R U?"

He responded, typing slowly with his thick fingers. "Fair. On a case."

Her response was instant. "Will meet U in 60."

His phone rang before he could respond.

"Detective, it's Bill. They said you should head over to the cattle barns.

Crime Scene investigators found something in Cuddles's pen."

"Tell them I'm on my way."

Thorson left St. Urho's and walked down Cosgrove, taking a shortcut behind the band shell and then a quick detour through the food building. After that last text from his ex-wife, he knew he needed more Fair food. He'd gained a good fifteen pounds since the divorce and planned to slim down soon. After the Fair. Until then, he'd eat well, hoping the food would absorb the acid that had built up over the past year.

He handed a couple of dollars to a girl wearing a foam cheese wedge hat and in turn received a greasy basket of hot, fried cheese curds. He ate them too soon and burned his tongue, but he knew he'd have to gobble them down quick as he trotted down Carnes Avenue. He almost stopped for a Reuben sandwich at Schumacher's but knew that would take too long. He turned south on Nelson, cutting through the DNR area and glancing quickly in the fishpond. In the shady depths, prehistoric looking gars and gigantic muskellunge floated silently. Nearer to the surface, rainbow trout flitted through the dappled sunlight. The water looked cool and Thorson found himself wishing he were floating in there with them.

He looked ahead and saw his next stop, the all-you-can-drink milk booth. The cheese curds had been delicious, but salty. Thorson paid the $1 and drank down three quick cups, finishing a fourth while he continued along Judson to the cattle barn. He wondered again, as he had when he first spoke to Lyle, how Cuddles could have made it all the way through the fair without anyone noticing.

He saw the crime scene tape around a pen near the entrance to the cattle barn. Posted outside the pen was a picture of Lyle and Cuddles in better times.

"I heard you found something here?"

A crime scene investigator with plastic gloves held up a clear plastic bag containing a bloody metal pie spatula.

"Ah. The real murder weapon?"

"We'll have to test it to be sure, but we are fairly certain that is not strawberry–rhubarb dripping from the edge. It was buried in the corner here under some hay. In a Fleet Farm bag."

Thorson remembered the ticket stub and fished it out of his pocket. He could just make out the writing on the back of the stub. It was a phone number. He jotted it into his notebook before handing the stub to the crime scene investigator.

He dialed the number on his cell phone. "State Fair Security," said the voice on the other end of the line.

Interesting, Thorson thought as he announced himself. He asked for a log of all the calls in the past 24 hours. "Were you on duty this morning?"

"Yep. We got that call around 7:30 this morning. The one about a bull in the Creative Activities building."

"What time does the building open?"

"That's the stumper. The building doesn't even open until eight a.m."

"Does Security monitor the building before it opens?"

"No. We're not sure how a person could have been in there yet, let alone a bull. They found a broken lock on one of the Education building doors."

"That's next to Creative Activities, right?"

"Yep. They're connected."

"Get the caller's name?"

"No, but we'll have the caller's phone number on the log. Possibly a name."

"You're in the admin building, right? Right across from Creative Activities on Dan Patch?"

"That's right, Detective. We'll get the log ready for you."

"Appreciate it. See you in about fifteen minutes."

Thorson had already planned his route back to the crime scene. A brisk walk north on Liggett would take him right past the Midway and to the Grandstand. On his way, he saw Nando just outside the funhouse with his bag of tools. He wondered. Had Nando hidden the pie spatula in Cuddles' pen? Thorson motioned him over.

"Take a walk with me."

Nando smiled nervously, revealing the nasty-looking teeth. "Sure," he said, "No problem." The detective and the carney turned at Carnes.

"Do you mind if we make a quick stop?" Thorson asked as they neared the corn on the cob booth. "Want some?"

"No thank you, Detective. Gives me gas." Another nervous smile.

Thorson methodically began eating the corn. "Mind if I ask a few more questions?"

"No problem."

"So this guy meets you this morning at St. Urho's before eight a.m.?"

"Right. After sunrise."

"You said he handed you the pie and some money?"

"That's right."

"What else can you tell me about the guy?"

"Not much. I guess he was just a regular guy. He was really dressed nice, that I can tell you. He had a nice blue suit and tie. Seemed like some kind of a businessman."

"A businessman?"

"You know—he had a cell phone clipped to his belt and he was wearing one of those fancy earpieces. He was talking on the cell phone when he got here. He was carrying a lot of stuff, I think that's why he unloaded the pie on me."

"What else was he carrying?"

"He had a whole lot of rope, and he had a big grocery bag that looked like it had some clothes in it. And he had another bag, I think it was a Fleet Farm bag. Kind of strange, a businessman with a Fleet Farm bag and a lot of rope."

Thorson finished his corn. A couple of girls dressed in old country costumes got Nando's attention. They wore sashes reading "Slovakian Dancers". Both girls were sturdy-looking blond farm girls. Nando nodded as they approached the corn stand. "Where are you ladies from?" he asked, sensibly keeping his teeth covered.

"Wadena!" one shrieked.

Her dairy-girl twin slapped her. "Joanie, don't be talking to strang-

189

ers."

"Want some free Midway passes?" Nando offered. "Got a one-eyed friend called Pirate Jack that runs the bottle cap game in the Midway. Go see him and tell him Nando sent you. You'll win the biggest animal he's got."

"See, Patsy?" the giggler shrieked to her friend. "He's nicer than he looks."

"Joanie!" Patsy said, slapping her friend again. "Our dads'll give us hell for talking to this guy."

"I don't care," Joanie said pertly, accepting the tickets.

"Stop by the funhouse, that's where I work. I'll find some more passes for you girls. Girls all the way from Wadena should have a good time at the Midway, I'll see to it." Nando winked and smiled at both girls.

"We definitely won't be seeing you," Patsy said as she took her cob and left.

"I'm not so sure about that," Joanie said, smiling at the ugly carney.

Thorson couldn't believe this murder suspect was such a flirt, as ugly as he was. But stranger things had happened today.

"Those girls were nice. What's Wadena anyway?" he drawled, watching the girls sashay away.

"It's a small town in northwestern Minnesota. Say, do you mind coming along with me? I'm thinking you might remember more if you saw the crime scene."

"Why sure!" Nando said enthusiastically.

Thorson was sure that Nando wasn't smart enough to fake that level of excitement. He was acting like a little kid who'd been allowed to stay up past his bedtime. A little kid with bad teeth and the hots for some farm girls.

A few minutes later, Thorson and Nando had made it to the State Fair Security building and Thorson had a copy of the call log in his hands. "Three calls between seven and eight. This one here is from the call about the bull being in Creative Activities. It's a local area code. They even have a name. Dierkins. Looks like another lead to follow up.

"Does that name mean anything to you? Dierkins?" Thorson asked.

"No." Nando scratched his chin, screwing up his forehead as he appeared to honestly try to recollect anything else. "You detectives sure have to put a lot together."

"Let's go to the Creative Activities building. I want to look things over again."

"I'll look things over, too. Maybe something else will come back to me."

Nando lifted his shoulders and kept up with Thorson, more energy in his step than Thorson had seen in him today. He'd gained a sidekick. Every cop needs his sidekick. But a carney with bad teeth? Thorson and Nando. He was hoping for someone more like Tonto or Robin.

Thorson's phone buzzed again. "My ex-wife," he explained to Nando.

"Ex-wife. I got a couple of those myself. What's she want?"

"She's here at the Fair. Come to collect her alimony." He texted his location in reply.

"Now you know why I got no permanent address."

Thorson smiled at Nando for the first time that day. "I'll have to consider that myself."

They arrived at the Creative Activities building entrance. The place was packed with fairgoers looking at display cases of handmade crafts, quilts, afghans, clothing, lamps, rugs, and toys. An elaborately gaudy bald eagle carving attracted Nando.

"Wouldn't you love that hanging over your fireplace?" Nando gushed, genuinely impressed.

Not really, Thorson thought. At the moment he was living in a tiny, cramped apartment. No fireplace, not that he'd want a bald eagle hanging over it if he had one.

Thorson led Nando through the handicraft displays all the way back to the food section. The crime-scene tape had been removed, along with the dead bodies. Ahead of them, Thorson saw Lyle Johnson.

"They carted Cuddles out back and loaded him on a trailer. They're going to take him over to the Ag school and cremate him. I couldn't stand to see that."

"Nando, this is Lyle. He raised the bull they shot for no reason at all."

"Sorry to hear that, Lyle. I'm sure he was a fine bull."

"Thank you, Mr. Nando."

State Fair officials had gathered near the pie display cases and were removing the pies.

"I heard somebody say they have to do the pie judging over since that winning pie was stolen."

The substitute judge was a thin bald man with a knobby Adam's apple and an intense expression. He wore a blue suit, and pinned to his lapel was an official nametag with the State Fair logo on it. He had a cell phone clipped to his belt and an ear piece.

Next to him stood a thick-set middle-aged woman, wearing large round white-rimmed sunglasses and dark lipstick. She was nearly hairless herself. She smiled primly, clutching a badly made knock-off purse.

The man held up a new blue ribbon for the gathered audience to see and placed it on the thick-set woman's pie. Thorson inched close to the judge, close enough to read the name on his name tag.

"Dierkins."

Behind Thorson, two familiar voices spoke, one after the other.

First Nando announced too loudly, "Hey, that's the guy. That's the guy that gave me the money and the pie. He's the guy who told me to put the manure at St. Urho's."

Then he heard his ex-wife's voice. "Arvo Thorson! I want my money. Now!"

Thorson backed up slightly and turned. Something flew by his face. Strangely, his ex-wife's face was suddenly covered with pie. The crowd gasped and Thorson swiveled back around to see the judge aiming another pie point-blank at him.

Suddenly it was the side of the judge's face that was covered in pie—the side that faced Nando, who smiled a victorious, gap-toothed grin at everyone present. The crowd booed.

Pies began to fly everywhere, aimed in particular at the dirty carney, who ducked for cover behind a display case of nut breads. Thorson stepped toward Dierkens, who was trying to steal away across the slippery, pie-covered floor. A chocolate cream pie flew onto the fat woman's head, the chocolate shavings creating the hairpiece she was sorely missing. A trio of lime pies creamed a set of elderly Swiss triplets. A middle-aged father took advantage of the mayhem and pushed his pouty teen daughter's face into a meringue.

Lyle attempted to run around the jam and jelly case and cut off Dierkens. Instead, Dierkens grabbed the boy and a pie spatula, aiming the pointed end at the boy's neck.

"Everyone back off or the boy gets it," Dierkens shouted. The audience screamed. The fat woman said, "Tony. Stop. This has gotten too crazy."

"Sweet precious angel Darleen, you have deserved this prize for years. Betty Bruckle cheated you out of it for years by giving the prize to her sister-in-law. I put a stop to that, for you, Darleen!"

Dierkens continued to back away in the direction of the rear door of the Creative Activities building. "Just keep away," he said, "and the boy won't get hurt." The door was propped open. Bright August sunlight streamed in, backlighting the murdering, crooked back-up pie judge and his hapless victim.

Suddenly, something blocked the light coming through the door. The crowd gasped again. Thorson mouthed something to Lyle.

The audience had gone quiet. Darleen stammered. "T-t-t-tony. S-s-s-stop! Watch out!" Dierkens became confused.

Dierkens swiveled around and Lyle slipped out of his grasp. "Cuddles?" Lyle said incredulously.

Dierkens was face to face with a 1,500-pound Black Angus bull that was supposed to be dead. It turned out he wasn't. And this time, he was angry.

Cuddles stepped forward into the room and cornered Dierkens next to the Gedney Pickle booth, pushing him over into a box of foam pickle hats. Lyle grabbed Cuddles by his halter and calmed him down.

"Cuddles!" He said. "You're alive!" He threw his arms around the black beast's neck.

Thorson stepped in and held Dierkens until the Falcon Heights police were back on the scene. They cuffed him and read him his rights.

"Darleen!" Dierkens called out to his wife, who was covered in chocolate cream pie and sobbing over her now-ruined knock-off purse.

"Darleen, I did it all for you. I got so mad that she never let you win even though your pies tasted so bad. That shouldn't have mattered. You worked real hard on them. So yes, I killed her. I got that bull to make it look like she'd been gored. I coaxed him all the way across the fairgrounds in the middle of the night and waited all night and all morning until security came. But who knew the damn bull didn't have horns."

He began to plead. "Darleen, can you ever forgive me?"

Meanwhile, Thorson's wife approached. She too was covered in pie.

"Go home, Helen. Just go home. You'll get your check."

She left, defeated and sticky with Darleen Dierkens' extremely awful strawberry-rhubarb pie.

Thorson approached Nando. "Good aim," he said. "And good eye for detail."

"Am I off the hook, Detective?" he asked.

"We might need you to testify, but yes, you are off the hook. Go get cleaned up for your Slovakians."

Nando grinned, and this time Thorson didn't look away.

Thorson had one more person to say goodbye to. And a bull to thank. Belatedly, an Ag department student vet had turned up. He shook his head after listening to Cuddles' thumping heart.

"He must have been stunned—the bullets ricocheted off his thick skull and left only a flesh wound. Other than that, he's as healthy as ever."

Lyle affectionately scratched Cuddles' massive neck.

"He's gone from murder suspect to hero, all in one day. He saved your life, didn't he?" Thorson said. "I guess that's what makes him a champion."

"You got that right, sir! Thanks for believing in him."

"You're very welcome, Lyle. And thank you, Cuddles!"

CROSSROADS DELICATESSEN PEANUT LOGS

Courtesy of Chef Scott Hill

INGREDIENTS

- 1 4 oz. stick of butter
- 1 10 oz. bag mini marshmallows
- 1 tsp. vanilla
- 1 10 oz. bag caramels

DIRECTIONS

Melt the butter and marshmallows together, then add vanilla. While still quite warm, beat in 3.5-4 cups powdered suger. Mixture should be stiff but pliable. Roll into pinky-finger-sized pieces. Freeze. Melt 1 bag of caramels in a bowl. Using 2 forks, dip the fingers of nougat in the caramel. Lift and tap off the excess caramel and immediately cover in roasted salted peanuts. Place on parchment or waxed paper. Ready to eat when the fingers have thawed (30 minutes).

About the Authors

KRISTI BELCAMINO is a Macavity, Barry, and Anthony Award-nominated author; a newspaper cops reporter; and an Italian mama who makes a tasty biscotti. She writes books featuring strong, fierce, and independent women facing unspeakable evil in order to seek justice for those unable to do so themselves. Her first novel in the Gabriella Giovanni Mystery Series, *Blessed Are the Dead*, was inspired by her dealings with a serial killer during her life as a Bay Area crime reporter. She is also the co-author of *Letters from a Serial Killer*, co-written with the mother of the girl kidnapped and killed by the serial killer who inspired *Blessed are the Dead*. Her first YA novel, *City of Angels* (Polis Books) came in 2017.

CATHLENE N. BUCHHOLZ is a freelance writer and former anesthesia technician. Her writing has been featured in *Festival of Crime*, *Tonka Times* magazine, and *Murmurs of the Past: An Anthology of Poetry and Prose*. In her spare time, she dabbles in the art of belly dance, performs karaoke, and practices target shooting on her private gun range. She is currently working on a series of suspense novels, set in the Twin Cities, with her cohort in crime, William J. Anderson. Cathlene lives on a hobby farm in East Central Minnesota with her family and a menagerie of animals.

MARLENE CHABOT, a semi-finalist in the 2016 Neoverse Writer's Competition, has been writing mysteries since 1995. Her freelancing career for magazines, such as *Her Voice*, and other entities in her native state of Minnesota began in 2007. She has a B.S. degree in education, an A.A.S. business marketing degree, and a certificate from the Institute of Children's Literature. Her other published writings include five novels— *North Dakota Neighbor, Mayhem with a Capital M, Death at the Bar X*

Ranch, Death of the Naked Lady, and *Detecting the Fatal Connection*—as well as three short stories for anthologies—"A Visit from Santa," "The Missing Groom," and "The Gulper Eel Lounge." She is a member of Sisters in Crime and Marco Island Writers.

TOM COMBS, author and ER physician, combines diabolical plots and murder with the blast-furnace emotions of authentic medical action and billion-dollar intrigue. He's authored two Twin Cities based thrillers, Nerve Damage and Hard to Breathe. He's a member of International Thriller Writers and Twin Cities Sisters in Crime.

CHRISTINE HUSOM writes two mystery series, both set in Minnesota: the Winnebago County Mysteries and the national best-selling Snow Globe Shop Mysteries. She has published stories in four anthologies, written a collaborative novel with eight authors, and co-edited *A Festival of Crime* for Nodin Press. Christine served with the Wright County Sheriff's Department and is currently a Wright County Commissioner. She is a member of Mystery Writers of America, and both the National and Twin Cities Sisters in Crime. www.christinehusom.webs.com.

SUSAN KOEFOD writes novels, short stories, and poems. Her Arvo Thorson mystery series debut, *Washed Up,* was praised for its "gorgeous prose" by Library Journal. Other books in the series include *Broken Down* (2012) and *Burnt Out* (2013). Her debut young adult novel, *Naming the Stars,* was published by Curiosity Quills Press in 2016. Short stories have appeared in *Ellery Queen Mystery Magazine* and in other print and online venues. She is a recipient of a McKnight Artist Fellowship for Writers. For more information, please see susankoefod.com.

MICHELLE KUBITZ is an ex-journalist and currently writes under two hats: one as a proposal writer in the IT industry and the other as a fiction writer who likes mystery with a dash of paranormal. Kubitz lives in southeastern Minnesota and has roots in the farmlands of northeast

Iowa. A member of Sisters in Crime and Mystery Writers of America (MWA), Kubitz previously received the Hugh Holton Award, recognizing promising new writers by the MWA—Midwest Chapter. Kubitz can be found online at www.michellekubitz.com.

LORI L. LAKE is the author of eleven published novels and two books of short stories and is the editor of three anthologies. Lori writes the popular Gun Series and the Public Eye Series. She and Jessie Chandler recently edited an anthology called *Lesbians on the Loose: Crime Writers on the Lam*, which won several awards. Her short work has been featured in *Writes of Spring, Silence of the Loons, Once Upon a Crime, 15 Tales of Murder, Mayhem & Malice*, and *Women of the Mean Streets*. She's known for sharing writing resources with both aspiring and published writers and is especially fond of teaching about the crime fiction genre. When she's not writing, Lori's at the local cinema, curled up in a chair reading, or teaching writing classes. Her next mystery release is the fifth book in the Gun Series, *Gunpoint*, due out in late 2017. She's currently working on a book about creativity for writers called *Sparking Creativity: Words of Wisdom for Your Writing Inspiration*. Her website: www.LoriLLake.com.

BRIAN LANDON is the author of the Doyle Malloy mysteries series, including *A Grand 'Ol Murder*, which was named Best Minnesota Mystery by Minnesota Public Radio. He is also a contributor to and editor of the holiday anthology *Why Did Santa Leave a Body?* He lives in Blaine, Minnesota, with his wife, Michelle, his son, Devin and daughter, Madison.

BRIAN LUTTERMAN is the author of Downfall, which launched the Pen Wilkinson series and is described by Mystery Gazette as". . .an exhilarating action-packed financial thriller . . ." His other books include *Windfall* and *Freefall*, the highly-praised sequels to *Downfall*, and *Bound to Die*, a Minnesota Book Award runner-up. Lutterman, a former trial and corporate attorney, writes cutting-edge corporate thrillers, bringing to life the genre's outsized conflicts and characters with breathtaking action and suspense. He lives with his family in the Twin Cities. Visit his website at: www.brianlutterman.com.

COLIN NELSON'S grandmother introduced him to crime mysteries by giving him a Sherlock Holmes novel when he was ten—he's been hooked ever since! Maybe that's what led him into over thirty years of working as both a prosecutor and a public defender. He's tried jury trials from misdemeanors to murders and has seen crime from every possible angle. Six of his books have been published, along with a collection of short stories. He has three different serial characters: a female prosecutor, Zehra Henning; a private criminal defense lawyer, Ted Rohrbacher; and an investigator for the U.S. Export/Import bank, Pete Chandler, who travels to crime scenes in many exotic locations around the world. He also plays the saxophone in a jazz group and a rock band. Married for over thirty years, he has two adult children.

MARILYN RAUSCH is the co-author of the Can Be Murder trilogy and author of two novellas. She enjoys cooking; her signature dish is Cranberry Chicken with Wild Rice. The mother of two adult children, she resides in Plymouth, Minnesota, with an overweight tabby named Kip.

MICHAEL SEARS' bestseller *Black Fridays*, a thriller with a financial twist, took the Shamus award and was short-listed for the Edgar and three other major awards. *Mortal Bonds*, the critically-acclaimed second novel in the Jason Stafford series, won the Silver Falchion at Killer Nashville. Continuing the series, *Long Way Down* was described as "one of the best thrillers of 2015." *Saving Jason*, fourth in the series, is currently available from Putnam. Mr. Sears was a Managing Director for two different Wall Street firms, where he worked in the bond market for twenty years and, earlier, in foreign exchange and derivatives. Prior to returning to Columbia University for his MBA, he was, for eight years, a professional actor. He lives in Sea Cliff, NY, with his wife, Barbara Segal, and the cat, Penelope. When not writing, he is frequently found sailing or enjoying the company of his new grandson.

NANCY TESLER is the Amazon-bestselling author of the Other Deadly Things mystery series, which introduces the reader to the murderously wacky world of divorce, where biofeedback stress reduction therapy is the order of the day. As Nancy has been both a biofeedback therapist and a divorcé with homicidal fantasies, she feels uniquely qualified to have written this series. *Pink Balloons and Other Deadly Things*, published by Dell, the first in the series, received a starred review in Publishers Weekly, and the fifth book, *Slippery Slopes and Other Deadly Things*, garnered a "Wow!" review from Janet Evanovich herself. Nancy has also been an actor, a soccer mom, and a playwright. Although three of her books are set in New Jersey, where Nancy raised her three sons and numerous animals, she now lives in sunny California with her very level-headed, newly-acquired husband and three rescue cats, which proves there is life and love after divorce. Her latest novel, *Ablaze*, an emotionally gripping thriller/love story, is a departure in genre from her previous amateur sleuth novels. Nancy is a longtime member of Mystery Writers of America and Sisters in Crime.

Dubbed by reviewers as the Queen of the Northern Gothic, WENDY WEBB is the bestselling and award winning author of four novels: *The Tale of Halcyon Crane* (2010, Holt), *The Fate of Mercy Alban* (2012, Hyperion), *The Vanishing* (2013, Hyperion), and her newest, *The End of Temperance Dare* (2017, Lake Union). Her books have been published worldwide, translated into eight languages, and are also available in e-book, large print, and audio formats. She lives in Minneapolis with her dog Zeus. She is at work on her next novel, which will be released in June, 2018.

RHONDA GILLILAND was voted Best Home Cook of October 1998 by the St. Paul Pioneer Press. She co-edited *Cooked to Death: Tales of Crime and Cookery*. She wrote, produced, and directed *Come and Get Your Love*, a Native American thriller , which was the 2009 winner of the "Audience Favorite" award at the Big Water Film Festival. She is a member of Sisters in Crime, MIPA, and Mystery Writers of America. Rhonda served as the Sisters in Crime Twin Cities' chapter president from 2012-2015. Rhonda is a foodie and has been a Yelper since 2008. A St. Paul, MN resident, she lives with her husband, a Russian Or-thodox Deacon, and tabby, Stryper.